Sexperience

FANTASY VS. REALITY

Dedication

For the person who does things without thinking,
then rethinks the situation once it is over.

Judgment is not for us to give;
it belongs to a higher power.

So, keep living life and
do what makes YOU happy.

Contents

Tow Truck Driver

It is hot as hell, and I am having the worst day ever. Everything that could have possibly gone wrong went wrong. Since I was low on fuel, I tried to preserve my gas by not using the air conditioner. Taking the 405-freeway home, traffic was tight, bumper-to-bumper. All the windows were down, and the sun had me feeling crispier than a Krispy Kreme donut. I ended up taking the local streets because it seemed like the fastest way to get home.

But while driving, there was only one thing on my mind—cumming all over one of my many toys from The SeKret Doors, an adult novelty store. What folks don't know is that they sell toys, lingerie, and anything you may need to spice up your sex life. They even host private events such as passion parties, paint, and sip events with female and male models. I have even witnessed them hosting a male baby shower.

Now back to the story. I am driving down Santa Monica Blvd, speeding near a residential street. I took a right turn, trying to beat the light. Little did I know I was heading into another disaster. I went over the curb and hit the light pole with my car's right tail end. To be honest, I felt like the pole hit me, but hey, everyone would still blame me anyway.

I could see it too, the moment they all turn and be like, "BITCH, IT IS YOUR FAULT!" Not knowing much about cars, I do what I do best–make a call and get ready to pay for good help. Now I am even more frustrated that I am in the heat, waiting on a tow truck when all I can think about is fucking the shit out of myself.

"I deserve to release some of this tension.
 I can't wait to get home."
I pouted and thought to myself.

After a good twenty-eight minutes and thirty-four seconds of waiting, I am ready to curse this tow truck driver out. They said he would be there in sixteen minutes, tops. Soon as he pulls up, he bounces out and reaches for something on his passenger side floor. I am talking shit as I reach for my cellphone and purse before getting out of my car. Never making eye contact, I start yelling.

"Look here, you fat nasty motherfucker."
Waving my hand in the air and rolling my neck,
"Y'all need to compensate me for this long-ass wait."

I was so focused on the stereotypical image of a tow truck driver in my head that I had him all messed up. A tall six-foot-something, handsome sexy chocolate man stood in front of me wearing Timberlands fresh out the box, dickie pants with a heavy crease, navy blue work shirt unbuttoned and abs poking out through his wife beater. His name stitched in blue and white, Armstrong, and baby, yes, those arms were strong, looking like The Incredible Hulk, ready to rip out of that shirt. The way his body glistening in the sun, I could not tell if it was sweat or body oil. He looked fresh from the barbershop with his lightly waved, tapered cut that lined up perfectly with his beard.

Oowie.

Mr. Armstrong was walking toward me. Then he was standing over me. Close enough that we could have shared a kiss. Mr. Armstrong was so tall that I had to look up when he opened his mouth and asked with a British accent, sounding just like Idris Elba.

"Excuse me, what was it that you said?"

Me and my stubborn attitude, walked past him slightly, rubbing my ass against his dick print, mumbling, "You heard what I said," I rolled my eyes and walked away.

Knowing how much a man loves a challenge, I had to maintain my hard-to-get mentality. Mr.Armstrong apologized multiple times for his tardiness. He had no idea that as soon as I saw his sexy ass, he was already forgiven. He checked on my car then informed me that it was still drivable. I would not need a tow, but he told me he would love to take me out to compensate me for the wait.

"I knew you heard what I said, but I guess that's a start," I smirked and rolled my eyes before handing him my business card, hopping in my car, and driving off.

With my day looking up, I headed home, not even caring about how much the repairs would cost me. I just got off without paying the tow truck driver, and I had an upcoming outing with that fine piece of chocolate. Mr. Armstrong had the potential to make my roster. I planned to have a lot of fun with him, and I knew exactly what toy I would be using when I got home. The wand was the perfect choice for the night.

I like to start it off slow then speed it up. I let it sit on my clitoris with a pillow on top while wrapping my legs around it. *Oh, yes.* I am picturing that man's tongue taking the place of my wand. I reach high levels of climax, while anxiously awaiting the actual experience. We had several conversations over the phone. Mr. Armstrong persistently asked me out on dates.

But, always putting my job first, I could not manage to pry away from work for too long. I let him come by for hugs and he brought lunch a few times. This one time he came by the job steady asking, "When can I take you out? I want to spend some real time with you."

I had made him wait long enough. It was time to see what that mouth can do in real life.

Loving to hear him beg in that accent,
I gave in, "Tonight."

Mr. Armstrong grinned from ear to ear.
His straight pearly white teeth had me wet already.

"What am I going to do with you?"
I asked.

"I know you have *plenty* of ideas already in your head."
He replied, and we both laughed.

We went to an elegant seafood restaurant for dinner. He stared into my eyes as we shared intense conversation, his fingertips skimming my lower thigh under the table. Not wanting to wait any longer, I grabbed his right hand and slid it under my dress. His eyes lit up, and with eyebrows raised, his lips curved into a smile. Surprised, but with it, his fingers jazzed around the tops of my bare thighs. My legs twitched as a chill ran up my back to my neck. He pulled my panties to the side and drew in a sharp breath.

Finding me wet as he reached my sweet spot, he gave a low growl of satisfaction. He began stroking my pussy with his two middle fingers while rubbing my clitoris in a circular motion with his thumb. Thanking *the Most High* for booths, I slouched down and used the table's base to prop one of my legs up so he could give me harder thrusts. By this time, I am feeling some of my essences run down my inner thigh and onto his hand. He pulls out and lifts his fingers to his mouth. I leaned in for a taste of myself as well.

Mr. Armstrong disappears under the table and gets to work. The long black tablecloth covers him perfectly. I concentrate on keeping a straight face and try not to moan too loud as people walk by, but the further we go, keeping quiet becomes the hardest thing in the world to do. Grabbing his head, I pull him in closer. We are both in too deep. I knew I had to stop him, even though I did not want to.

I pushed his head back and whispered,
"Fuuuuuck! Come up for air, baby."

He eased his way back up, grinning as he licks his lips and wipes his face just in the nick of time because the waitress suddenly appears.

"Is everything okay?"
She asks.

"Check, please?"
I reply.

We leave the restaurant and head back to his place since that is where I left my car. We pull up, and before he can take the key all the way out of the ignition, I had climbed on top of him. Slowly kissing, rubbing, and grinding on him, feeling his dick greet me through his pants. I do not recall how, but he got me out of the car while still attached to his body. I was not the thinnest thing on the shelves, so that turned me on even more. This strong mother fucker was about to get it.

We are still at it as we make our way inside. Taking each other's clothes off, licking, sucking until I am more than ready to start fucking. He fumbles for a condom, and I pull a magnum out of my purse like, *Baby, I got you.* I am attempting to put it on for him until I realize that is not his size... at all. I had given him *way* too much credit.

Now all types of thoughts are going through my mind. It is standing up, but maybe it's not all the way up. WTF? Where is the rest of it? Somebody please come get your son. You have got to be freaking kidding me. Is Ashton Kutcher about to jump out, yelling that I've been Punk'd? Let me get my shit and go. But wait... that head game was fire. I should at least see what Shrimp Dick can do.

While all this is going on in my head, Mr. Armstrong must have felt my vibes. To gain my focus back, he starts licking my neck, then eases his way down to my nipples. Mr. Armstrong slowly sucks then rolled his tongue down my stomach, where he kisses my inner thighs. He slides that tongue back inside of me. It is even better than the first round.

Okay, Lil Baby, I guess I'll let you finish. He put on his size condom and proceeds to slide inside with my legs throwing up the peace sign as he gripped my ankles, knowing exactly which way to stroke it. My knees are at my shoulders, and that shrimp is growing inside of me. It went from a shrimp to a hot dog, all the way to a hotlink...busted open. He was doing his shit. Baby fucked me like he had a point to prove. I loved every bit of it. I guess it is true what they say, it's not the size of the boat but the motion of the ocean.

Best Head Ever

All-Star Weekend in Las Vegas, and we are about to be lit. Everyone is familiar with the slogan "What Happens in Vegas, Stays in Vegas." Hopefully, it would stay that way. I am with my family and friends. We were having a good ole time, drinking, and walking the strip when we bump into an old friend name Monte and a ton of his guys. He had some eye candy with him.

Decisions, decisions.

A few of them I would consider taking down, but I locked eyes with a sexy one that stole my attention. Before I could speak to him, another one of the guys with tattoos all over his face walks toward me.

"What's good, baby? What's your name?"

"Tara, but I'm not going to waste your time. I cannot fuck with you. I refuse to be seen in public with you and all that crap on your face. It's like you are asking to get banged on. You're more of the Netflix and chill type of guy, and I'm looking for more in life."

"I respect that," he laughed.

Fuck the rest of them, I turned my attention back to *him* then added a smile and a nod. I wanted him. He was smelling so good. Flawless taper with small curls. Fresh plaid button-up, nice jeans, and some clean shoes. Monte and his guys were all kinds of dressy. So, I figured they might be going to one of the clubs.

He is blushing as he walks toward me.
My name is Taye" as he reached for my hand.
"Tara" as I extend my hand.

Small talking, Taye tells me he plays college football in Virginia, and he has one son. I let him know a little about me, too. We had so much in common. Especially our smart, sarcastic mouths. He could take a joke and knew how to make me laugh. I decided to keep in touch. He was someone I would not mind bringing back to California.

We never got the opportunity to see each other after Vegas. As time went by, we would talk for hours. Every chance we got we would call, text, Tango, Skype. Between classes and work shifts. On one of our late-night conversations, Taye hit me up, letting me know he would be in town. We agreed we were going to be taking things slow.

Once Taye made it to California, he stopped by his mom's place to visit his family, and afterward, he asked where I would like to go. I explained that spending time with him was all that I wanted. Just to chill with him while he settles in. We ended up at Taye's friend's house on Main Street. Everyone is chilling, sipping, listening to music, and joking.

"Come here," Taye grabbed my hand,
"I want to talk to you."

I followed him as he led me into a room. He grabbed my waist and sat me on the bed then knelt in front of me. Grabbing my hand, he looks into my eyes.

"You know I have to leave in the morning, and I won't be back until the next holiday break. I want you to wait for me. I will send for you to come to Virginia whenever you are ready, whenever you want. Just behave and wait for me." That was not a problem because we had gotten close over time. Although we still had not taken things to the next level, I did not mind waiting on him. Taye got me, he understood me, he knew me, and the feeling was totally mutual.

"I want to give you something to think about while I'm away," he was still kneeling before me, looking into my eyes, "Something that should help make your wait a little bit easier."

I was confused as fuck. What could it be? We had not known each other long enough for marriage. Or had we? I was nervous as chills went up my spine and neck.

Taye gently pulled me forward with his thumb touching my tragus and the remaining four fingers grabbing the back of my head. I closed my eyes as I leaned in for a kiss. His lips were as soft as mine with the right combination of moisture and tongue. I was so wet simply by a kiss. I was thinking to myself that maybe it was time. He must have had me under a spell or something.

Taye stood me up while our lips were still locked, then undressed me. Each time he took a garment off, he gave that area his full attention. I am talking about kisses from head to toe. Literally. It was like he was writing on my frame with his tongue. He was such a gentleman, catering to my body as if they spoke the same language. I did not have to guide him at all. I am fully undressed, and Taye's admiring my body. Complimenting every angle.

Every scar, mole, stretch mark, my thighs, my pretty toes, the freckles in the middle of my back, my smooth skin, my dimples, even my birthmark. Taye begins to go down on me, licking as he spreads my pussy lips wide. Rotating his tongue around my clitoris, passionately sucking as he looks me in the eyes. I am holding back, trying not to cum in his mouth. Yet and still, I cum repeatedly. I could not control my nuts. He is slurping, licking, sucking and having my legs going crazy while he eats it.

My body is getting weak. At this point, I have lost count. I could not tell you how many times I came. Hell, I did not even know I could cum that many times at once. I am at a loss for words. I am his dinner and his plate. He must have been hungry. He ate it all and then started washing the dish with his tongue. I am literally trying to speak, but I have developed cottonmouth or something. I am dehydrated. That man had sucked the fluids out of my entire body–all of it.

Taye was good!
No, Taye was GREAT!
No, TAYE WAS IMMACULATE.
 That was THE BEST HEAD I'D EVER HAD!
I have NEVER had head like this. I think I am in love.

As he is licking and sucking my soul out of me, I hear music. I do not know if it is playing in the next room or only in my head, but I hear Jill Scott's *He Loves Me*, and his tongue moves in rhythm with the melody. What could I do to thank him? Should I give him some head? Nah, I would not be able to top his performance. I could let him fuck me, but I am so weak he might think I cannot hang. Hmm, I could just ask him what he wants. Fuck it. I would let him have whatever he wanted.

I push his shoulders back, lifting his head.
"What about you?"
My question is spoken in a whisper.
He moaned as he replied,
"This is for me, I'ma eat your pussy until I nut."

I did not know if that was good or bad, but I was guessing that he does not nut quick because he had been going for a while. I did not know if I had anything left in me. Taye has eaten me to the point where I am repenting and praying for him in my head. "Lord… forgive me for all my sins, known and unknown, and thank you for blessing this man with the gift of talking in tongues. Thank you for the bond that is being built between my body and his. May we have many more like this. In the name of the Father, the Son, and the Holy Spirit. Amen."

I am loving what Taye is doing and if it were to show me what I'd be missing if I didn't wait. Then, hey, point proven. If I got that treatment every time he left, then I want him to leave regularly. It was the type of head that would have me tripping on anything I thought might come in between us. I was not losing him. The head is to die for.

Fuck that, in my mind; we just got married. What shall I name our future kids? I mean, he seems like a good father to his son. Hopefully, the dick will complete this package. If so, I might propose to him. He grunts while giving a long passionate moan, as he strokes his dick allowing his cum to flow out. I am stuck and still speechless. I would have opened wide to catch that. Better yet, write your name with it all over my body. Oh no, I am too weak to talk. Maybe next time.

Game Night

It was Wednesday evening, and I received a text from Karter, a playmate of mine, or what some would call a "fun boy". No matter the day of the week, he was always down to party.

Karter: We're having game night. You should come through.

Me: Okay. I'll be there in about an hour.

Just getting off work, I showered and changed from my business attire into something more casual and head over. Everyone is greeting me as I walk in when Karter's cousin, Meko, yells out, "Aw, shit, his partner in crime, "Falsetto," is here. We have to watch them 'cuz they be cheating." Everyone laughs.

"Why you call her Falsetto?" Meko's friend, Tina, asks. "You'll find out before the night is up. Just watch," he laughs. "We don't cheat. We just get each other," I say in my defense.

"Riiiight. He is hating because we always beat him," Karter adds, "Now we about to make his ass get sloppy drunk."

"For real," I nod my head and smile.

We played every drinking game you could think of; King's Cup, High Card/Low Card, Never Have I Ever, Speed, Jenga, Twister...Everyone was winding down and intoxicated. Meko, Tina, Karter, and I were the only ones left standing. The four of us were sitting on the couch, talking, joking, and reminiscing.

Karter and I make eye contact. He gave me "the look." The *I'm bout to fuck the shit out of you* look.

I was smiling as I ease my way to his room. He waits a couple of minutes and eases his way out of the living room. As soon as he closes the door, we immediately get to kissing and undressing. Rough sex. No holding back. He picks me up, and I am riding him as he leans against the wall. I am hitting all types of high notes as he was banging my brains out. Sounding and feeling like a porn star. Everything is feeling so good until we were interrupted by a knock on the door.

"What the fuck!
Don't stop, Karter,
you better keep going,"

I tighten my legs around him. Karter follows my directions and keeps on pounding inside me, even when the door opens, and Tina, and Meko walk in, he never breaks his stride.

"Do y'all want some competition?"
Tina raises an eyebrow.

Karter looks into my eyes, and we laugh as he throws me onto his bed then slides back inside of me. My moans grow louder and louder. Tina and Meko lie down on the bed beside us and begin to have sex. Tina is moaning. It was like we were making a harmony together. Karter and I liked spicing it up and trying new things, so having an audience was not a problem at all. The fact that they thought they could compete with us was hilarious.

We continued screwing as if Tina and Meko were not there. Karter spreads my legs, and pushes them over my head as he is stroking deep inside me. He loved my flexibility. My left leg is so close to Meko's face that he grabs it and starts rubbing it as Tina is riding him.

"Ride my dick," Karter groans, and I climb on top and start riding him, squatting on my tippy toes, and rotating as I bounce my ass up and down.

"You know Daddy like that shit!"
Biting his lips and gripping my love handles.

"I know you do, baby,
and I know what you like even more."
Running my tongue down his earlobe.
"Give it to me then."
Giving me a smack on my ass.

I spin around while his dick is still inside of me. I spread my legs into a Chinese split position and begin bouncing while moving from front to back. Not bothered by the fact that I have my legs across Meko while Tina was riding his face. This position gets Karter every time.

"Dang, girl," Karter body strained
to stiffness as his penis throbbed inside of me,
"If I didn't have a condom on, you would've
definitely got me doing that."

Karter tries to regain control by getting on top and forcing me into my favorite position. He is deep stroking, knowing sometimes I can't take all of him like that. Sliding back, or in his words, "running from the dick" until my head and upper body hang off the side of the bed. All the blood rushing to my head mixed with a cock rush through my guts has me about to explode. I am trying to hold my cum in, but I still feel some coming out.

"Yeah, that's right.
Cum all over Daddy dick.
This is your dick!
This is home for us!
No matter what,
we always find our way back."

He grabs me by my waist and flips me over before starting hard thrusts from the back. He is beating it up, and I'm throwing it back until I can no longer hold it in.

"Ooh, shiit, fuuck…
I'm finna come…
Ooooo, baby…
Umm, Ooo, baby, baby…
Oooo…"

I felt two sets of hands smacking me on my ass. I look back to see, it was Karter of course and Tina. She and Meko had stopped their session and was enjoying the show.

"Now I know why they call you Falsetto,"
Tina gives my ass a final smack
We all laughed as we stood up and got dressed.

"Oh, and for the record Tina, I'm my own competition."

I tighten the muscles in my butt cheeks making my booty jump from right to left.

Call It Quits

I had been dating this guy named Joshua for a couple of months, and it totally was not working out. He wanted to force something that did not fit. I am trying to go with the flow, but the vibe just was not there. He was a genuinely nice guy, but just not the guy for me. I was kind of dodging him because I was ready to end it. Joshua keeps blowing my phone up, so I finally decided to answer.

He asks me to go to a bar with him because it was his friend's birthday. He insists on picking me up around 9:00 p.m. I figured I would go just to end things on a good note. As we were drinking and eating, I keep trying to ease in the break-up conversation, but he cuts me off or changes the subject. On top of that, his friends are there, so he always has an excuse to walk away.

At the end of the bar, I noticed an old playmate, KeeKee, and how he keeps eye-fucking me. Finally, Josh comes back to the table, and I tell him.

Me: "Look, I can't do this. You are a great guy. Just not the guy for me. We want different things right now, and I do not want us to hold each other back or slow each other down. I rather we go our separate ways, and just do us."

Josh: "I knew this was coming,"
Josh grabs my hand.

Josh: "Can we still be friends?
Maybe you just need some time."

Me: "Yeah, that's fine. I have to go,"
 I grab my purse and start to stand up.

Josh:"Noooo. Stay, please.
Friends can still hang out."
Josh's suggests with a long face

Me: "True. Okay," feeling at ease and
awkward at the same time, I sit back down.

Josh gets back to parading around like everything is okay. In a way, I guess it was. KeeKee and I locked eyes again. Steady smiling. I could not resist. Eventually, I give him a nod as I grab my purse and head to the ladies' room. I do a sweep to make sure it is empty and send him a text. Soon after, he joins me and locks the bathroom door behind him.

KeeKee bends me over the bathroom sink, and I raised my dress while he rips off my panties. I am trying not to be too loud, but it is not working as I realize how much I missed his dick. I was not thinking about him before, but the way he was digging in my guts had me reminiscing about our old days.

I turned around, kissing him as he picks me up. I lock my legs around him as I ride him. Grabbing the edge of the counter for extra support, he is gripping and stroking me as if he missed me just as much. KeeKee bends me toward the counter with my head against the mirror as he sucks on my breast. I feel his dick giving massive throbs, and we are both about to cum at the same time. Knowing that, I began grinding and bouncing faster and harder to get it all out. Gripping his dick with my pussy.

There is a loud BOOM, and the sink hits the floor. Water comes flowing out–along with our nut. I pulled my dress down and walked straight out of the bar. KeeKee follows me. I get in his car, and we ride giggling as he drives me home. The next day Josh calls me asking why I left without saying goodbye. I told him I started my period and had to hurry home.

"So that was you who used the sink as a shower in the ladies' room?" He laughs.

"What the fuck are you talking about?"
I put the phone on speaker.

"No beautiful. I'm only kidding.

I guess after you left, the ladies' room flooded.
They said someone broke the bathroom sink, and water went everywhere."

"Nahhh... That's crazy, though.
I wonder how that happened? But I'll hit you later."
I hang up the phone as me, and KeeKee die laughing.

Your Time Is Up!

Dealing with Tommie's bull crap had become annoying. We had been going nowhere for a while. I saw potential in him that he did not see in himself. When I tried to guide him to something positive, he made it seem like I was trying to be his mother. All I wanted was growth. I only pushed him to do the things a man should want to do, like buy property together, get his own business started, and find ways we could make more money.

I had connections with brokers and higher, paying jobs but he was happy just making a minimum salary. It seemed like he was comfortable with not having much. I was building myself up. Since we were supposed to be growing together, my goal and job as a woman was to help build him up, too. I am sure I was not the only one who had lusted over a person they knew wasn't meant to be in their life. Over time, they see no growth in the "situationship"—yet they cannot find it in themselves to leave because it is never the right time.

If you find yourself at this stage, LET IT GO. You are blocking both of y'all blessings. Do not get me wrong Tommie and I had our good times. He was handsome, sweet, fun, outgoing, spontaneous, and he provided when he could. Things had eventually gotten to a point where anytime I said something, he was quick to call me a parole officer. He said I needed to stop checking in on him and that I needed to give him time to figure out what he wanted to do. I had been calling, texting, and trying to make plans with him, but he had pushed me away, claiming he was busy doing something. It sounded like a half-ass excuse, but I got the point. I was too convenient. I had always made myself available whenever he wanted or needed me.

So, I gave him what he asked for—space. It had been weeks since we last talked. I stop calling just to say "hi" or to check on him. I had even stopped being his alarm clock for work and his reminder for appointments. It seemed like we were growing apart. I could not say that I did not miss him, but I was loving my new lifestyle and being able to focus on myself. I was eating better, saving more money, accomplishing goals, and meditating more. I was really in a good place.

Months had passed, and I still had not heard from Tommie. I started dating a new guy named Dre. He knew all about my previous "situationship." Dre was amazing. He had so much ambition that he inspired me. He motivated me to do even more. He was highly intelligent, sweet, an amazing listener and paid attention to detail. Like the time we were out eating at a restaurant near the mall. Full after the delicious food, we decided to walk around the mall to burn a few calories. Dre was showing me items and asking my opinion on various things.

We are complimenting one another as we discover multiple shades that look good on us and played around in stores. I did not mention it to him, but I saw this beautiful anklet that I knew in my head that I might return for later. We continued to joke around, picked out a few things, and went to my place. We started watching a movie and once the movie came to a romantic scene, I began tearing up.

Dre pulled out the anklet I had seen earlier.
Dre: "Your eyes twinkled as you gazed at it."

Me: "You are so thoughtful. Thank you."
I reach in to hug him.

Dre: "It is made of amethysts—your birthstone and
it would match the dress you bought a few
weeks ago when we were out."

Me: "You are a hopeless romantic,
just like me, and I loved it."

Halfway through the movie, Dre went into the kitchen and came back with some stuff I did not know I had ingredients to make. It was ice cream with cookie bites, drizzled with something sticky like honey, and slightly browned with cinnamon or chocolate. I am not sure, but I do know it was good! Did I mention he was creative, and he can cook? He started feeding me the ice cream. When a funny scene happened in the movie, we were laughing, and a little fell on my chest. Before I could reach for a napkin, he had already set the bowl down and licked the ice cream off my breast.

As he is sucking and licking my left boob, I am already anticipating his next move. He unbuttoned my blouse and bit my right nipple through my brassiere. I lifted, allowing him to unfasten my bra with a single try. He is sucking, kissing, and licking my stomach, tits, and around my belly button as I'm easing my blouse and undergarment completely off. He pulls my skirt and thongs down as I lift my ass in the air to assist.

He grabs the spoon and begins drizzling
 the ice cream on my pussy.

Me:"I guess you're not done with your dessert,"
I trail my hand down his arm.

Dre: "I made a mess on you. I better lick it up,"
Dre twirls his tongue .

Me: "Ummmm,"
I rest my head against the couch.

Dre: "I'm just getting started and
I was raised not to leave nothing on my plate."

Me: "Oowwiiee," I gasped.

Dre's tongue is deep inside my ocean. I am soaking wet and trying not to run from the hard thrusts of his two fingers plunging into my vaginal walls. My legs tremble as he licks my yoni from all angles. He grabs my thighs before lifting me up and sliding me down to the edge of the couch. He positions himself so that he is kneeling in front of me. *All Hail the Queen.* I felt like royalty.

Me: *"Oh, my God!"*
I whimper.

Dre: "Yeah, that's right,"
Dre murmured softly.

Dre: "Call his name and thank him
 for blessing you with this good, pretty pussy."

He is smacking and twisting his tongue in quick motions around my clitoris as I moan and giggle.

Me: "Let's not forget he blessed that mouth, too."

Dre: "That's right. Now we both about
 to be talking in tongues."

Dre continues to stroke my pussy with his tongue. Up and down, round and round. The feeling is amazing. Out of nowhere, my phone rings. I don't get calls after hours unless it is Dre, and I was already with him. So, I looked to see if it was family or a friend calling with an emergency. I was surprised to see that it was Tommie. I declined the call and put my phone on silent. Dre looked confident as he smiled. He knew he did not have anything to worry about. He had my full attention. Soon he was sliding inside and passionately sexing me. Seductively staring into my eyes as he is licking and kissing on my body.

Meanwhile, my phone is vibrating like crazy. Tommie has *never* called me, and I did not answer, so he was probably on the other side of the phone going insane. But it was no longer my concern anymore. Dre fucks me like he is madly in love with me. Sometimes we made love, sometimes it was rough sex, sometimes it was a quickie. Our vibes indicate the type of sex we were going to have. Right then, he was on passionate lovemaking, but as my phone keeps vibrating, I can feel the change in him. I am digging it. It was turning into rough passionate sex—that *I have a point to prove* kind of sex.

After a while, my cell stops vibrating, and I hear Tommie's voice. I had no idea how my device somehow got answered. Next thing I know, someone is at my door. Not a gentle knock but pounding like they are the police. I am in my zone. Anyone who knows me knows that I am a screamer if it is really good. Sex with Dre was always good. Dre had my ponytail wrapped around his left hand as he is smacking my ass and grabbing my waist, digging deep from the back. I can feel him in my heart as I am leaning over the arm of the couch. I glanced up at the window and saw a male's silhouette.

"You a trifling hoe ass bitch! No closure or nothin'. Open the door. I'ma kill both of y'all bitch asses!"
Tommie's voice in rage from outside. I chuckle as Dre keeps at it.

Dre: "You my girl.
Tell him who pussy this is."

Me: "Yours, baby!"
I scream.

Dre: "Say my name,"
Dre plunge into me deeper.

Me: "Ooh, Dre...
Baby, don't stop."

Dre: "Tell that fuck boy to get up outta' here."

Me: "You gotta' gooooo!"
I shout as I begin to bite into the throw pillow.

Dre: "Fuck outta' here, bro,"
 Dre smacks my ass.
"Your time's up!"

Tommie: "I'ma catch y'all slippin',"
Tommie gives the door a loud thud.

As Dre and I reach our climax, we hear glass shatter. Before we can throw some clothes on, I hear a car burning rubber. I did not want to look. When we went outside, we saw that this fool done busted our car windows and drove off. All because his time is up.

Reunited & It Feels So Good

I had a huge crush on a guy I went to high school with named Lee. He was close friends with my male best friend. He was handsome, smart, pretty ass teeth, and always into something. The whole bad boy demeanor. But my best friend always kept my head focused on school. Telling me to concentrate on my education.

"We are young. Guys only want one thing from girls.
Do not rush it."
He told me repeatedly.

I respected him so much that I did just that. Fast forward to fourteen years later, and guess who I bump into? Yes, Mr. Lee himself. Normally, I was not into guys with hair, but his dreads were looking nice—black fading into brown, with a clean taper. Smelling good, looking good, and he still had those pretty ass teeth. We catch up over dinner, and for some reason, I did not want to let him go. I wanted to have sex with him so bad. All I could think about was how good his dick game might be. I had to find out. I was not in high school anymore, I was grown.

Lee: "I don't want this night to end," Lee gazed into my eyes. "I know a spot we can go to in Hollywood. You wanna roll?"

Me: "Sure, I'm in no rush to head home."
I looked away. Trying not to appear anxious.

Lee: "Cool."
He gives a cunning smile.

Lee pays for dinner, and we hop into his car. We were driving on the i101 west, and traffic is tight. Everybody is trying to get to their destination. I am so horny, and I cannot hold it in. I had contemplated in my head different ways to say, "fuck me now... I want this dick." Out of nowhere, my courage comes out, and I blurt, "Fuck me now!" My eyes got buck wide. I was in shock.

That must have been music to Lee's ears. This man pulls over on the side of the freeway and did just that. I laid flat on the passenger side seat. My pussy was dripping. Soaked through my panties. He had pulled them to the side and was sweating as he pounds my pussy. No need for me to fake this orgasm. I was spewing all on his dick. He is fucking me hard and fast, then nice, and slow.

Lee: "Come here. Sit that pussy on my face,"
Lee grabbed my waist as we switched positions.

Me: *Fuuuuuuck!*
Where had he been all my life?

Lee is lying in the passenger seat, and my legs and feet are in the back seat as I am riding his face. My toes are curling. *Here comes another one.*

Me: "Ooh, myyy Gaaawd!"
my legs are trembling.

Lee: "You taste so good, girl."
Lee is smacking and licking slurping,
knocking this pussy back,
it feels like his tongue is vibrating.

"Hold on... I gotta thank this dick."

He is lying flat on the passenger seat as I move into the 69 position where I am upside down and on top of him. I am kissing and passionately licking up the length of his long brown caramel dick. Absorbing my cum that I had left on it. He was right; I did taste good. I reach in between his legs to my purse and pull out some honey to try a little trick I learned from my ex. I drizzled some honey along the sides of his shaft, then cleaned up my mess with my tongue, swallowing all our juices. Sucking as it rises to the tip. I rotated his balls while licking his chad with slight sucks periodically until his leg begins to jerk.

Lee: "Come here, ma,"

Lee attempts to lift me up. But I am no fool. I had him right where I wanted him, and he was about to cum hard.

Me: "Umm-umm,"
I am shaking my head as I moan and keep sucking.

Talk about making a woman squirt.
This man skeet all in my mouth.
 I just swallowed it like a champ and kept going.

Once again, Lee attempted to regain control, but I was not going for that. I got on top of him, sitting on his lap as we both face forward. Leaving the passenger door open, I let my right leg hang out because it gave me a better balance as I rode the life out of his dick. I'm bouncing, ass smacking, and clapping, then next thing I know, flashing lights are everywhere and not white. They were red, white, and blue. We were about to be arrested for indecent exposure, though I thought I looked pretty decent riding Lee's dick!

Quick Layover

On a flight home from Ohio, the plane had to make an emergency detour and land in Texas. The flight attendants notify us that we would be stuck in Houston for six hours. Something about them needing to switch our plane at the last minute and having to wait on the new one. Contemplating my next move, and the time needed to get back through TSA if I leave the airport, I could not resist the urge.

I decided to hit up Kevin, my "Super Man" to let him know I was in his part of town. There was something about looking into his eyes as his tall, stocky, mean, stubborn ass stood over me. He has those big strong arms like Dwight Howard. He made me feel secure and untouchable. I felt like no harm could ever come my way when he is around. Any who... he was so thrilled. I could hear the excitement in his voice as we talked. He placed me on hold, then immediately arranged for his driver to pick me up and take me to his spot.

I complimented him on his nicely decorated house. He had remodeled since the last time I had been there. Before I could start a new sentence, I was in his arms, and he was hugging me, squeezing me, and kissing me as if he *really* missed me. Kevin starts to undress me as our lips are still locked. Shoving me against the wall. Kissing my abdominal area and making his way down to my pelvis. He placed each of my knees over his shoulders, as he devoured me, making me weak. I slid down as he squatted to lift me properly. Still eating my pussy, Kevin is standing tall as I crossed my legs around his back with my thighs clenching around his neck.

Kevin: "I can't breath."
He chuckles while tossing me on the bed.

Me: "Sorry."
I moaned and giggled, attempting to curl up.

Kevin: "Unh-unh, come here."
Kevin grabs me by my ankles and
pulls me to the edge of the bed.

We made passionate love all over his house. Blessings every room as he caressed my body like he was massaging me and rocking my world at the same time, catering to my body's every need. He had gone to get me something to drink and prepare a quick meal as I laid across his bed and eventually dozed off. I woke up to him kissing my inner thighs, then he inserted his tongue into my vaginal walls, giving me heavily seductive strokes. He slides that chocolate dick inside of me, and I melted all over again.

He fucked me nice and rough that time. I grabbed his dick, ready to thank him with some good head. As I give the tip a kiss, my alarm goes off again. We had already hit snooze a few times prior. I knew I could not afford to miss my flight. I had an important meeting once I landed. I jumped up and grab my things, throwing my clothes and shoes back on. Kevin grabbed me by my waist as I was trying to head out the door. I was in a hurry to get back to the airport before I missed my flight.

Kevin: "Wait, my driver will take you back."
Kevin mumbled as he passionately kissed my neck.

Me: "It's okay. I scheduled a Lyft. They're outside already." I call over my shoulder as I'm running out.

No time to even freshen up. I had to wait until I got through TSA to go to the bathroom and take a birdbath. It was well worth it. As we boarded the plane, Kevin called me to see when I would be back.

Me: "I'm not sure."
I smiled as I tilted my head to the side.

Kevin: "I'll send for you soon."
Kevin replied alluringly.

Me: "Okay."

Placing my phone on airplane mode, I slid my tongue across my lips. I could still taste him. I closed my eyes, wishing I would have had a little more time to continue that groove.

Curiosity Killed the Cat

Growing up in Compton, I had dibbled and dabbled in a few hoods, hanging out with friends or sometimes on solo missions. I had made a name for myself in a positive way. So, I was well respected and felt safe wherever I went. The goal had always been to make it out the hood, but we always found our way back. Years pass, and social media makes it possible to keep in contact with those I did not get to see often. The "People You May Know" feature also allowed me to explore new faces. I am scrolling down my timeline, laughing at memes, and watching funny videos when I eventually realize that I have a direct message.

Daddy134pl: You look familiar.
Where do I know you from?

Me: You don't know me.
If you did, you would know from where.

I am confused because he does look really familiar. I check his profile to see that he had posted a video over the last 24 hours showing a close-up of his face. Where did I know this man from? Better yet, who sent him? On his story, he has his shirt off and looks like he just got done working out or something. I got to see some of his tattoos and physique. He has a huge marlin fish with an F on his chest that resembled the Florida Marlins logo.

I am learning a lot about him without him having to tell me. He was obviously from Front Hood Compton Crip. Getting a tattoo that big, he better be about action. You cannot deny your hood with a tattoo that big, but I can tell he reps it proudly. He has his sleeves done, but I cannot quite see the details, but the way he is capturing my attention, I will know soon enough. He is not all ripped and cut up, but he was not fat and flabby either. His arms look nice and strong. I love nice arms, especially with the veins that poke out enough to outshine any other visible body part. He was very much workable. So, I doubled back and replied to his story.

Me: So, you flexing sending out thirst traps?
That's what you do?

Daddy134pl: Nahhh believe me I'm not doing that at all.

Me: What's your name?

Daddy134pl: Rendale.

Me: You went to Dominguez?

Rendale: No, I went to Compton High.

Me: I must admit you look familiar. Maybe I have seen you at a block party or something in your area.

Rendale: Maybe so.

Me: You know what... maybe it's best that we don't know where we know each other from.

Rendale: why you say that?

Me: I don't catch bad vibes. Everything is energy with me. I'd know if it was a bad face. Plus, I would like to have some fun with you and wouldn't want anyone to mess that up.

Rendale: You don't have to worry about that.

Me: I hope not. I'll take your word for it.

Rendale and I continue to converse and flirt over time. After watching his stories, I see he spends a lot of time with his daughter and son. He was growing his hair out, it looked kind of attractive. I was not into guys with hair any longer than waves or a fade. He was in school, trying to make something of himself. He did not post any females or SeKret dates. Like how some people will post the food, location, and drinks but NEVER the

43

person they are with. One thing I could not stand is a guy who hid or does not claim his woman or children, so I saw a little potential in him.

His latest post was a video of him leaving his house, jogging down a set of stairs with a gallon of drinking water. He was wearing some grey Nikes sweatpants and a sweatshirt that was unzipped with his chest out. Of course, I checked out his print. It was pretty much all I noticed—dick bouncing after every step he took. If I had not seen his black and white Ralph Lauren briefs as his pants slightly sagged, I would have sworn he wasn't wearing any. I slid in his DM's, replying to his post.

Me: You flexin'.

Rendale: I'm not. I'll show you flexin' if that's what you want to see.

Me: Let me see.

He went idle, minutes turning into hours. Maybe I had run him off with my shit talking. I did not have a filter and just be popping off sometimes without thinking. Of course, I could back it up, but I did have to get better at picking my battles. I was lying in my bed when I received a notification. It was a DM from Rendale. He sent me a video of him in his king-size bed. That man knew his angles. The reflection from his mounted TV gave just the right amount of light as he strokes his dick up and down, slow, and seductively. It was shiny and perfectly veined. He had big muscular hands, so the fact that there was more dick left after wrapping his hand around it let me know he had length. What really got me was that his grip did not completely fit around his dick. *That mutha fuckah is phat and long*.

Oh, hell noooo…I need my kitty cat to still work after him. He was not even my *forever* guy. I would be crazy to have sex with him. I had seen those girls in the strip club whose pussy lips look like chitterlings that had been dragged on cement. You know what I'm talking about. That pastrami pussy. I am sorry but as pretty and perfect as his dick looked, I was not touching him.

I left him on read for a couple of days. I had to get my mind right. Man… his dick was perfect though; all one complexion, glazed cinnamon brown, thick with the perfect mushroom head and the right number of veins. Nope! No, sir! Consider this confusion and our conversations… DONE! I had finally reached my verdict and responded back.

Me: I need my walls sir. I cannot do nothing with you.

Rendale: It is not that big. The camera adds pounds to pictures.

Me: Nahhh boo-boo. I am not crazy and who ever can take that without any issues is a beast. I salute any woman who can.

Rendale: You crazy

Me: You are laughing but you know I'm dead ass.

Rendale: I know.

A few months pass, and we were still watching each other's stories and conversing periodically. I miss our flirty, nasty conversations, but I am terrified of this man. I am tempted yet scared of his dick. What if he breaks my pussy? I have heard stories about loose pussy. I cannot be in that category. Fuck that! I did not care how handsome and charming he was. I could not do it. But I missed my buddy. I don't talk to many people, and I believed we were great company.

Let me be honest. I wanted to *fuck*. Like I really, *really* wanted to *fuck* him. At the same time, I cannot help but imagine how his dick was created. They say, "God don't make mistakes," but I think he was overly blessed. Or maybe God had been overwhelmed and interrupted while creating this man. As if God gave him body parts directing himself like, "Chest, waist, dick, hips, thighs..." then got interrupted mid-body.

God: "This person's about to commit another sin, I gave them multiple signs, and they still ask for more." Then He doubled back like, "Where was I? I think I was at dick. Fuck it, give him more dick."

I did not know what the cause might be, but I did know he was the cure. I knew it was going to hurt, yet I wanted to try it—bad. Just one time. Hopefully, curiosity does not kill the cat. Literally. I told my buddy that I wanted to see him. Without hesitation, he invites me over. As I'm bathing in the tub, I am giving my pussy a pep talk.

"Look here, I know this may seem like intentional pain, but maybe it will not hurt as much as I am guessing. We rarely get to have some fun. If it hurts too much, I promise I will stop him. This dick I am about to introduce you to seems magical. It is so beautiful. It's all one complexion. It is long, so it may go pretty deep, and it is thick, so it may hurt a bit, but don't worry, I won't let it stretch you out. One time should not do too much damage. If he is not doing it right, I promise to stop him in his tracks and either take over the situation or end it completely. I just need you to show up and show out. Let us have Rendale right where we want him. We cannot be intimidated by his look and size. We got this, okay?"

I arrived at Rendale's house around 8:00 p.m. He has dinner prepared. The food and Rendale smells nice. I head over to check out the food, and his stove. This will let me know if I am eating the food or not. His home was well maintained. Exceptionally clean, and the decor was nicely arranged. A little too formatted. Cute but possibly done with a woman's touch. So, I excused myself and went to the restroom. I checked to see if there were any tampons or pads under the cabinet, feminine soap in the shower, and to count toothbrushes. There were only three, his and one for each of his children.

Me: "Okay, you passed a couple test." I sipped my wine. "I have to make sure no female lives here or will come busting through the door at any given time."

Rendale: "Come here." Rendale escorts me to his room and he opened every drawer, his closet, and gave me a tour of the house. "No one lives here but me and my children on the days that I have them. I do not bring females to my house. I don't trust nobody. It is something about your energy that makes me feel like I have known you for years."

I believe him. He was very convincing, so I relaxed, and we prepared to eat. He made shrimp and broccoli Alfredo pasta covered in parmesan cheese with garlic bread. Not bad for a bachelor.

Me: "It was delicious," as I wipe my mouth, "I'm proud of you. I was expecting a spread or something of that nature."

Rendale: "Oh, you have jokes," Rendale snickers.

Me: "Just a few."

Rendale puts on some music as we head over to the couch. We talked for a while. He is being a perfect gentleman, but I did not come here to chill. I came to award my curiosity. I am trying to see what that elephant trunk do.

Me: "I'm going to use the restroom." I see him watching my ass as I walk away, so of course, I add a little switch to my hips.

Freshening up in the bathroom and putting on a lingerie piece I got from The SeKret Doors collection. A red lace thong, bodysuit with a spaghetti strap over the shoulders, and a small strap across the back. I keep on my black six-inch heels and oiled up a bit more. As I walk into the living room slowly, I see his eyes light up, astonished. He was not expecting what he saw. He stood up to approach me once again, and I pushed him back on the couch. I climbed on top of him and kissed him on the neck. I slowly began to run my tongue down his earlobe, and I can feel his dick growing under me.

Me: "Is that a gun in your pants, or are you really happy to see me?"

Rendale: "Trust me, the gun is always close but, you just woke up a sleeping dragon."

Rendale picks me up and lies me on my back. My legs are spread. One leg hanging over the back of the couch and the other hanging toward the floor. He lowers himself between my legs and begins kissing and licking my neck down to my breasts. He caresses one as he sucks the other before pushing them together and licking and sucking them both.

Me: "Whatever you do to one, you have to do to the other. Treat them equally. I don't want lopsided knockers."

Rendale: "I got this!"

And that he did. He was writing cursive with his tongue on my stomach, over my laced lingerie as he made his way down. He pulled the thong to the side as he ate me for dessert. He then eased the lingerie off me only to go back and eat some more. My juices are flowing, and I am more than ready. He whips that big work of art out and grabs a condom from his pants pocket. As he puts it on, I gasp, thinking aloud.

Me: "It's even bigger in person.
 What the hell did I get myself into?"

Rendale: "Just trust me. I'll be gentle," Rendale whispers, "I was born with this. I know how to use it. I promise I won't hurt you."

Me: "Okay, but do I need a safe word or something?"
I place my hand on his chest as I brace myself and he laughs.

As he eases it in, I feel like I am losing my virginity all over again. He feels much bigger than I have had in the past. This dick could really hurt someone if not used properly. My body is tensing. He knows it is hurting but's being very gentle and continuously asking if I'm okay. He pulls out periodically to comfort my pussy with his tongue, attempting to ease the pain before sliding back in. Great pleasure mixed with a bit of pain. It is bittersweet. The odd part was that I really enjoyed the pain. I had a high tolerance for it.

He is stroking me slowly as he grabs my thighs, looking me right in my eyes, and I am gazing right into his. He pulls out and picks me up and carries me into his room as one would carry a bride over the threshold. Laying me on the side, he opens one of my legs as he slides back in. My left leg folds while my right leg aims for the sky. He is deep inside me as he rolls me to my back. We adjust so that we are chest to chest. He is still stroking me as I suck on his neck. Getting deeper and deeper.

My sucks turn into bites. Rendale turns me to my stomach, raising me by my waist, and gives my pussy more pleasure with his tongue from the back. Sliding back in, gripping my hips as he eases my ass up a bit more. He smooths a hand down the arch of my back. Trying to be a big girl, I try to slowly throw it back. Why on earth did I do that? It was like he took it as a challenge, and his strokes became harder and a bit faster. Moaning loud and clenching my teeth as I rotate and throw it back. Fuck that. I could not let anybody out do me. My moans turn into screams that I am hoping the music would drown out. Pleasure and pain never felt this good.

Me: "Slow down, your dick too big."

Rendale: "Awh... fuuuuuck... I'm about to bust." Rendale moans.

Silently thanking God because I did not know how much more I could take.

Me: "Ooooh, my God, right there..."
 I give out a loud moan.

He plunges his dick inside me a few more times, and I am taking the pain. It hurts so bad but feels so good. We both come, and he pulls out.

Rendale: "Tara, you're bleeding." Rendale yells.

Me: "What the heck! Are you serious?"

It was nowhere near time for my period, so I hopped in his shower, embarrassed and scared. He came knocking on the door.

Rendale: "Are you okay?"

 Me: "No," I sadly reply.

Rendale: "Can I come in?"

Me: "Yeah."

Rendale gets in the shower with me and washes both our bodies from head to toe.

Rendale: "You're still bleeding."
Rendale gives a concerned look.

Me: "I'm going to stop by the emergency room."

Rendale: "I'll go with you. Does it hurt?"

Me: "A little. It burns like a cut when it gets wet."

We got out of the shower, and he gave me a shirt, some briefs, and basketball shorts to wear. I had a pad in my purse, so I put it on. We were waiting in the fast track area at the hospital when the nurse calls me to the back. Rendale gets up to go with me.

Nurse: "Is it okay if he comes with you?"
The nurse asks.

Me: "Yes. He's the reason I'm here."

The nurse looks confused as we both laugh.

Nurse: "What brought you here today?"
The nurse leans on the counter as she opens my chart.

Me: "We were having sex, and
I think he broke my quannie."

Nurse: "What do you mean?"
 The nurse asks.

Me: "We were having sex, and after, we noticed that I was bleeding."

Nurse: "Let me take a look." The nurse examines me and then pauses. "Ooh, I see."

Me: "What do you see?" I lift my upper torso, leaning on my elbows.

Nurse: "I see you tried to force something that doesn't fit." She starts making googly eyes and smiling at Rendale, "You ripped a small tissue. Nothing that a few stitches cannot heal. Also, I recommend no sex for a while."

She is still smiling at Rendale as I am putting my clothes back on. He looks at me, and I look at him, and we both start laughing.

"That is all you, nurse.
Just be careful.
Curiosity may kill the cat."

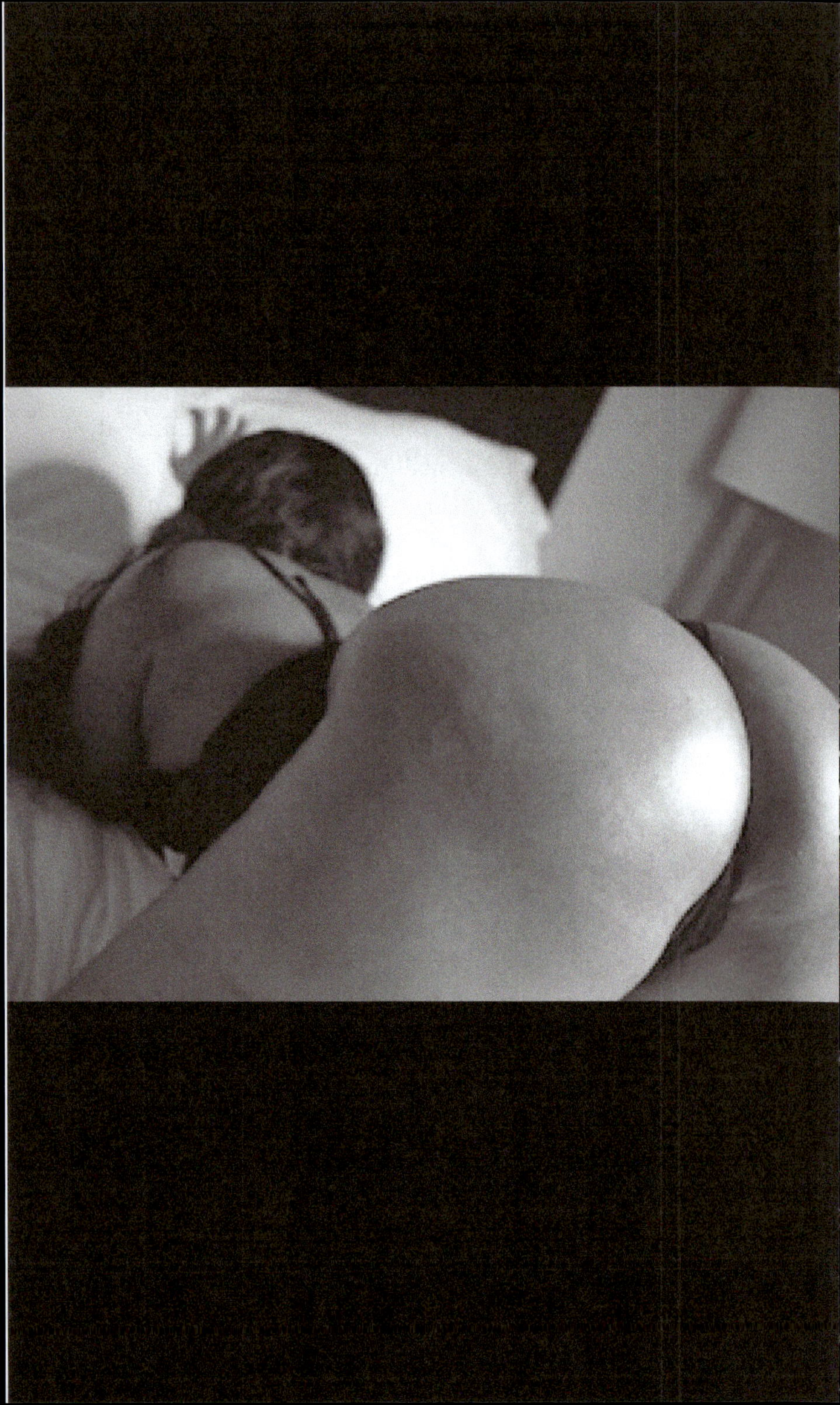

Airbnb / Uber Driver

I worked hard, and I deserved a break. Miami was not sounding too bad. I preferred the urban style of travel. I wanted to mingle with the locals, eat authentic food, and spend a little time in the hood. Resort life was too easy. You rarely left the property because they had everything there. I did not want to do the tourist thing, so I searched until I found the perfect spot on Airbnb. It had a jacuzzi bathtub, private patio, and was only five minutes from South Beach.

Clubs and great restaurants would be nearby, plus it was 420 friendly. Not that I smoked, but I might meet a Haitian guy down in Little Haiti to bring home with me. Rumor is, they like to get high. Right before I confirmed my booking, I needed to see what my host would look like. I did not want a creepy, yuck mouth guy like the movie, *13 Cameras*, watching me. Ugh!

I click on the icon to maximize the image and see a nice piece of eye candy. He has the whole beach scene in the background, both arms behind his head, giving a nice smile with straight teeth, beach shorts on with a white V-neck shirt. He did not have the perfect body, but those teeth, his arms, and that sexy face were a turn on by itself. I immediately confirmed the home. Once the reservation was confirmed, I received an instant message from a guy named Michael, thanking me for booking and saying he looked forward to my visit. I responded with a simple 'thank you.' I plan to fly out Thursday morning just in case I felt a little jet lagged. I would be able to rest the first night and turn up Friday full of energy.

Wednesday night approaches, and I am all packed up and ready to go. My business is in travel mode, which means it will still run while I am away. I catch a 6 a.m. flight straight to Miami and then take a cab to my Airbnb. When I arrive, the host, Michael, is there to greet me. He compliments my beauty and tells me I have really great skin. I thank him and ask for recommendations on good bars or clubs, and the best places to get authentic Haitian and Cuban food. He directs me to Wynwood. Then Michael let me know for a small fee, he can be my personal driver for the weekend. I took his number just in case. After he leaves, I prepare to hit these Miami streets. On my way out I walk past the jacuzzi yelling,

"I brought some waterproof friends just in case I continue to be a good girl on this trip."

I called an Uber and head out on the town. Miami was amazing. I went to a place called Coyo Tacos, a restaurant that had a night club in the back. Super dope. I headed straight to the bar, got a double shot of Don Julio. I am enjoying myself as I dance and mingle. Just having a ball. There must have been something about my Cali swag that has got these guys going crazy. They are buying me round after round, and I feel my buzz kicking in. But a good girl knows her limit, and I have had enough to drink for the night. I walk to the front where the tacos are served and ordered my food. When I reach into my clutch, one of the guys who was buying me drinks at the club reaches in to pay the cashier.

Me: "I could've paid for my food and my drinks."
I laugh.

He smiles as he says, "You look like you could've, but I wanted to.

Me: "I bet you want to do a whole lot more," I responded in a slur. "But you aren't getting no booty for that."

He tilted his head and gave a smirk as the people surrounding us all laughed. Knowing what he wanted and knowing I was not about to give it to him, I decided to call an Uber and head back to my Airbnb. Two minutes later, I am heading to the front, looking for my driver. What a coincidence to find that it is Michael, my Airbnb host. I guess it was meant to be. I reached for the door and got in the car. He keeps looking in the back seat, smiling from ear to ear. I laugh it off and finish the last few bites of my food and lick my fingers. I can see him steady peeking through the rearview mirror, so I give him a show. After cleaning my hands with wipes from my purse, it's game time!

I moan softly, spreading my legs, cocking them open just enough to give him a slight peek. I touch my breast, rubbing and squeezing them as I rotate my tongue, licking my lips. I start playing with my pussy in his back seat. Michael acts cool for a while, driving slowly as if he is trying to make the show last. When his facial expression begins to change, I can tell he wants in so bad! We were at a stoplight with no cars behind us. I peeped how he let the light turn green, yellow, and red—multiple times. We are both enjoying it as I go to work on my pussy. Licking and sucking my fingers as I push them as deep as I can back inside me. Baby was in a daze, looking both confused and anxious.

By this time, traffic is piling up behind us as horns start blowing. We are about a block or so away from the Airbnb when he grips his long thick, dick, and begins stroking it. I keep going, almost at my climax, moaning loud until we were responding to each other's noises...

Me: "Oooh...Shiiit! Fuuuck..."
Biting my lip as I lift up, penetrating harder and faster.

Michael: "You like that, baby. You want me to give you some more?" Michael grunts as he continues to yank his cock.

Me: "Give it all to me, baby. Don't stop.... This feels so good, I'm about to cum."

Michael: "Oh no, I don't wanna nut. I want this feeling forever. I want you, girl."

Me: "Ooooooo," I moaned one last time as I squirted all on his back seat.

I get more wipes out of my purse, clean myself up, and attempt to take care of the mess on his seat.

Michael: "It's okay. I'll take care of that," as he holds his cum in his right hand.

I get out of the car and start walking into my Airbnb, knowing Michael wants to have sex with me.

Michael: "Wait!" Michael yells out. Sticking his head out of the car window.

Me: "For what?" I look back laughing

Michael: "Can I come in?"

Me: "No, I already came." Continuously laughing as I enter the door.

I went inside and locked the doors. It may be his property, but he was not invited inside. So, I kept my taser and mace close, just in case. He was still sitting outside as I got ready to get in the jacuzzi. The thought of him giving me a bad review had crossed my mind, but I realized that I did not care. I got out of the hot tub and slept like a baby that night.

Love In The Club

It is Saturday evening, and with no events planned at the shop for the night, I am thinking about heading out with my ladies. We could hit up a lounge, sports bar, or something. Nothing too fancy. I call my bestie and let her know I'm stepping out and to see if she wants to link up. By the time I reach home, I am greeted with a sexy aroma. Daddy is fresh out of the shower and smelling like a million bucks. I want to take him down right then and there, but we had different plans for the evening. I still stole some kisses and copped a few feels.

He smacks me on my ass and chuckles, "Babe, chill, you already know wassup. This is our cheat night, so behave."

"Alright, Daddy, you got that" I laughed.

He left to go pregame with the fellas since they were doing their own thing.

Soaking in the tub, with my music playing on shuffle. I am about to be on my worst behavior as I put on one of my "get em girl" dresses, skipping the panties.

Oh, yes. That is right. It is cheat night. Occasionally, my man and I get to meet strangers and have sex with them, no strings attached. It has been healthy for our relationship though I do not recommend it for everyone. So, do what is best for you.

The girls and I decide to go to some random club in Hollywood. We are having a good time. The ladies are looking gorgeous as ever, and the fellas are spiffy. Great people, great vibes, and great music. The DJ was playing ALL the jams. Let us not forget great drinks. The bartender knew just the right amount of liquor to put in those glasses. I am feeling the scene, so you know I am feeling myself. Guys are hitting on me left and right. I am steady turning them down, still looking for the right one. My cheat night choice must be worth it.

I must admit I was enjoying the attention, though. I loved that feeling. I call it "Tara'Rella." It is when I go out, be as stunning as I am, flirt a little bit, dance, and give them a tease. When they ask for my name or number, I walk away and leave them looking for me. It never failed that one of the girls would call me the next day like, "Do you remember the guy wearing so and so? He was looking for you and asked for your number." I am never interested, though, just out for fun.

I decided to venture off from the girls, "I'm going to the bar, babe," I give my bestie a wink, and she smiles, knowing I am up to no good.

I approach the bar and order another double shot of Don Julio, easy ice with pineapple juice. Handing my card when a sexy voice from behind me says, "Put that up, I got it."

Before I can look over my shoulder, his sexy fragrance hits me. Baby smell so good. It was a mixture of soap and expensive cologne. He grabbed me by the waist and whispered in my ear.

Him: "Life without you is like a broken pencil... it's pointless."

I know what he said was cheesy as hell, yet it was still sexy. By this time, I am buzzin', and I know I will replay what he said in my head later. He is still behind me as we face the bar, grinding his dick on my ass, and it is feeling nice. With no room for error, I am hoping he will be my victim for the night. I got to see what his face looks like.

As I turn around, his friend walks up and says, "Bro, you know your girl crazy. You better tighten up."

Me: "He good," I reply, turning around slowly.

"Oooh, shit," his boy puts both his hands up and steps back slowly, "My bad, ma."

Me: "So, is your girl here?"
I trail my fingers down his chest.

Him: "Nah, she out with her friends."

Me: "Cool, I don't like drama, and I'd hate to beat yo' bitch up."

Him: "Watch your mouth, Lil' Mama," he uttered as he placed his index fingers to my lips.

Me: "My bad, Lil' Daddy!"

Him: "That's Big Daddy to you."

Me: "Prove it."

He grabs my face in an aggressive yet sexy demeanor. We share a passionate kiss, and the heat from my body feels like the whole club is watching us, yet I did not give a care about anyone but him. It was as if only him and I were in the room.

Him: "Can I have this dance?" Big Daddy takes my hand strolling me toward the dance floor.

Me: "Can you keep up?" I winked as I two stepped to the music, and we both laugh.

We dance to song after song, eventually finding a spot in the back of the club. Low key but still visible. The DJ must have read my mind. He started playing Usher's *Love in this Club*—and that's what we had planned to do. I eased the hem of my dress up in the back, and he had unzipped his pants. Kudos to the wise person who put a hole in briefs. We were getting it in on the dance floor, and I did not care who was watching.

"Girl, look at them," a female voice whispers, sounding envious, "She don't even know him," then other females giggled.

Knowing I had an audience, I wanted to show off by throwing it back even harder and rotating in a circular motion with every bounce. I could see that he wanted to give it to me in a wild way, making my ass jiggle and pop while he gripped my waist. Holding my thighs in a twerk position. I knew they could hear the claps from my ass as I threw it back. Somebody was probably recording us. *(If you are reading this, that was me, send me the footage. Please, and thank you.)*

He grabs my neck while he is still inside me, raising my upper body toward his chest and licking my ear.

Him: "I'm 'bout to tear that ass up, follow me," he whispers.

Big Daddy did a wiggle, squirm, and a double hop as he zipped his pants. I looked back, smiling, and flickering my tongue at the gossiping females, giving them a wink as I let him guide me through these tight places in the club. We walked down a long hallway, passing lines of people waiting for the bathrooms. He gave some guy a handshake that turned into a handoff. My guess was that it involved money.

"Last door on the left," the guy nods down the hall.

As soon as we enter the private room, I am all over him, kissing and running my tongue down his chest. I unzipped his pants and pulled out that big, mouth fulfilling, organic cocoa dick. Kissing the tip first, as it deserved special treatment, then massaging his balls as I lick the side of his shaft. I sucked the soul out of it until I tasted his sweet cum going down my throat. As his ocean is still flowing, there is a knock on the door.

A beautiful thick brown skin female walks in, her body looking like a reflection of mine. She grabs me by the hair, pulling me away from him. I swallow what was left in my mouth. She shoved her tongue down my throat and start to caress my body. I feel extremely aroused. Big Daddy wraps his arm around me from behind, trying to gain back my attention, bending me over while he slides his dick inside me. He begins to pound my soul with every ounce of love in him, and at the same time, she gets on her knees and starts licking my clitoris and sucking the pouch of skin that hangs below Big Daddy's penis and hold his testicles. She lay on her back as I soothe her cherry.

We ease down to the floor, with Big Daddy still inside me. I ride him as if my life depended on it. She leans in licking, feeling, and sucking all over our bodies. Then gives me "the look" as if she wants to take a ride, so I hop on board to his journey of the tongue, facing her and slow grind in a circular motion. She places a condom on him as she passionately rides his roller coaster. I place my hands around her neck, drawing her closer to me as our lips lock. Kissing as I came in Big Daddy mouth. We both continue to ride, speaking in French, her body trembles as she screams *je suis sur le point de jouir.*

Everything gets intense, real fast. At least that is what it felt like. We were at it for a while, I was loving every moment. As we were leaving the room, Too Short's *It's Time to Go* was playing. They had already done "last call" for alcohol. It was, indeed, time to go. As I am thanking our thick, gorgeous guest who showed up and showed out, his friend greets us in the hallway,

"Y'all some crazy ass freaks. Tara, your best friend waiting for you by the bar."

I gave my man a kiss and asked him if he wanted me to bring him something to eat on my way home. We met

back up at the house, and as we were discussing the fun
we had, we were at it again. I love my man!

Becoming Submissive

I am a boss in all aspects. At home, at work, in traffic, you name it. No matter the situation, I am always in control. People do not know how bad I have longed to be submissive to the right person. Being submissive to the wrong person could lead a fuck boy into believing that they are more than they appear, so it was important to choose wisely. Never let a fuck boy feel like he finessed you out of your pussy. Which brings me to a Royal story.

I had been talking to a guy named Royalty and trying to see where his head was at. Not to necessarily shape and mold him, but to introduce him to something he had never seen. With a name like that, it was easy to believe he should be catered to like a king. Off the bat, I gave him special treatment. I started calling him, "Dad," and I told him he had to earn stripes for the title of "Daddy." I had been teasing him, and I knew he wanted to fuck me— bad. I wanted our first time to make a statement, so I made him wait.

I started out by giving him the authority to make decisions for me. Like choosing what color panties and bras I could wear and the polish color for my manicure and pedicure. Then I moved on to asking permission to do simple things while making him wait for the full sexual experience. Tease him with passionate kisses, licking his neck and chest. Even grinding on his dick at times. I had bigger plans for him. He loved it, hoping to soon work his way up to sexual things like...

"Can I suck your soul through your dick, Dad?"

"Dad, can I ride it, please?"

"Can you fuck the shit outta me, Dad?"

I'd always been the type to allow a man to be a man, but shit hits different when you're willingly complying as a submissive. I gave him the upper hand on things I knew damn well I did not need his permission to do. Yet, for some reason, his dick would get super hard, and he was ready to fuck like a porn star when I made him feel like he was in control. Not only was it for him, but it was also for me. I wanted to know how it felt to submit. Who wouldn't want that?

His job required him to be away often, so when he called to let me know he'd be back in town around noon, I told him to get the room, and I'll meet him there around five. Royalty called to say he had a work-related emergency, but he would not be gone long. He had stashed the room key for me near the ice machine. I took the extra time as a perfect opportunity to pack some extra goodies in my overnight bag.

I showered and put on a two-piece lingerie set with a leash around my neck, then threw on my long black cover-up and tied it. I wanted to be ready in case he made it back to the room before I got there. I arrived before him and set toys in different places. My black and platinum double hearted paddle was on the nightstand, and I hung leopard handcuffs across the headboard. Bottles of watermelon flavored massage oil and apple-flavored deep throat spray were on the other nightstand. I'd brought the gag ball just in case, but that evening we could be loud as we wanted. My phone rang. It was Royalty.

Royalty: "Hey, love. I'm pulling back up to the room shortly. Do you need anything while I'm still out?"

Me: "No. All I need is you, so hurry up and get here."

Royalty: "I'm pulling up now."

Minutes later, I hear a motorcycle, and I peek out the window to make sure it was him. Anxiously, I watch him walk toward the hotel entrance and begin to blush. I throw open the door, and step back. He walks in to find me greeting him on my knees, a leash hanging from my neck and looking up at him. He reaches for my leash, pulling it toward the bed before letting go. He slowly runs his hands down the seams of my teddy, then wastes no time removing it.

Starting from the top, he strokes and sucks my breast then lays me on the bed. He is smooching my ribs and making his way down to my belly button as he slides the rest of my lingerie off. Still kissing my body making his way down south, he gives my inner thighs a peck as he spreads my legs. He licks my pussy then gives it a quick blow. Royalty reaches for the handcuffs and attaches me to the headboard, then blindfolds me, leaving me to imagine what will happen next.

Royalty: "Let me know if it becomes too much."
Royalty kisses my forehead.

Me: "Okay," I inhale deeply

Royalty turns on some music before he starts with the massage oil, rubbing me and licking me all over. Then he went to the ice, running it across my nipples as it melted. The anticipation was making me tense, not knowing if I would be feeling something warm or cold, wet, or dry. Royalty starts French kissing my pussy, instantaneously making me moan. I could feel him rotating his finger inside me while his tongue dominates my clitoris. I had nowhere to go, so I am squirming. He smacks my thigh with the paddle.

Royalty: "Stop squirming and take it."
Royalty demands as he gives another whack.

He rubs his dick up and down, along my pussy lips before he slides it all the way in. After he strokes me a couple more times, he places his right hand around my neck. With a firm, passionate grip, he begins deep stroking until he is pumping hard with no remorse, literally beating up the pussy and moaning louder than I am. I feel his body tightening, and his dick is beginning to throb as he pounds me. Royalty must not realize he is gripping tighter and tighter around my neck. Trying to take it like a champ, I give him several more seconds. Any more time and I would have blacked out. Luckily, that was the end of round one.

Without delay, Royalty collapses on top of me, looking like he is about to pass out. I had to remind him to uncuff me and to remove my blindfold, then I let him rest. When it was time for round two, I woke him up with a light kiss on the head of his dick. Swirling my tongue around and around, deep throating it as much as I could. Gagging and slurping as we made eye contact. Rotating my hand up and down as I juggled his testicles with the other hand. He was immediately intrigued.

He turned me until I was on my stomach, then placed me back in handcuffs. He reached for the double hearted paddle and smacked me on each of my ass cheeks. He put down the paddle and slid inside me as I willingly tilted my ass up. He grabbed me around the waist with his left hand and spanked my ass with the paddle in his right. I threw it back as he thrashed harder and harder, making me scream louder and louder. Dropping the paddle once again, Royalty slid both hands over my ass and up the arch in my back. He held on to my shoulders, riding me from behind like a horse in the Kentucky Derby.

I am looking back at him, locking eyes as he grabs my neck. He is stabbing me harder and harder. I am bouncing my ass on his dick with everything in me. He slows down, taking slower and deeper strokes. When he releases the cuffs again, I take it as an acceptance. Royalty was ready for Tara to take back her throne. I got on top of him, grabbing his neck as I ride him. Up and down, round and round. No surrendering. His body stiffens. Royalty is grunting and holding me. Squeezing me tight as he kisses on my tattoos. I can feel that he is about to cum, so I give him more bounces then jump off, gripping his shaft and stroking it. Right on time! As he is ejaculating, I am aiming it toward my face. Leaving him speechless, he looks at me with admiration and leans in for a kiss.

Royalty: "You are so sexy and nasty as fuck."
Royalty squeezes me tightly.
Chuckling as he embraces me.

Know Your Role

As I am driving to Terrance's house, my phone is ringing non-stop. It was in my purse in the back seat, so I could not answer it, and the Bluetooth was not connected to this car. I had used Terrance's car that day while he took mine to get fixed. I was stopped at a light when I finally reached for my phone. There were four missed calls and multiple text messages from Terrance telling me to call him ASAP, to hurry home, and that he wanted to talk to me about something.

I had immediately assumed something went wrong with my car while it was at the mechanic. Worried, I am speeding to get to Terrance's place. I see a cop car, so I pump my breaks and slow down to the speed limit. I dropped my phone in my lap so the cop would not see it. I am trying to call Terrance, and he's not answering. The cop pulls up alongside me and rolls his window down.

Me: "Fuuuck!" I roll my eyes.

Cop: "Roll your window down," the cop makes the motion, and I crack my window. "What's your name?"

Me: "Am I under arrest?" I put my hands up .

Cop: "No, I wanna get to know you." The cop blushes in admiration.

Me: "Don't you people come with wives and children?"

Cop: "You people?" He laughs.

Me: "Just because you're black don't make you one of us. You chose what side you wanted to be on."

Cop: "Give me your number, and I'll explain why I'm on this side."

Me: "I don't want to know that bad."

Cop: "Give me your number, or I'll give you the ticket I owe you for speeding and not having a hands-free device."

Me: "I knew you were foul. I smelled the bacon from over here."

We both laughed. He just bullied me for my number. He was cute, but still a pig at the end of the day. Anyway, back to Terrance...

Finally, he answered, panting over the phone.

Terrance: "Hey, ma. I can't talk. I'm a little tied up right now but be sure to meet me at the house by 9 p.m."

Me: "I'm on my way! Are you okay?"

Terrance: "Yeah, but I'll see you in a bit."

Me: "Okay."

Not realizing the cop was still driving beside me, I immediately dropped my phone in my lap again. Do not want to be bullied out of anything else. I rushed through the door, only to find that Terrance was not home, but I could smell his cologne lingering. I tap the back of my phone as I pace the living room. "What the hell, dude," I sigh, "He told me to be here by 9 p.m. It's already 9:18 p.m."

I'm about to get my ass in the tub. I'll see him when he gets here.

I was in my zone. Sitting in a bubble bath, with aromatherapy eucalyptus candles lit, and 90's R&B playing softly in the background. After a long day of work, I had to find a way to decompress. This was my sanctuary. While rinsing off I hear Terrance's keys jangling as the door opens. Anxious to know what all the fuss is about; I wrap a towel around me and greet him in the living room.

Terrance: "Ma, we've been talking about another threesome for a while. I'm ready."

Me: "Fool! This is what the emergency is all about? Your ass could've waited until I got home to talk about this," I laugh, feeling relieved, "Maaan, I thought something drastic and bad had happened to my car or something."

Terrance: "Nah, nothing like that. But do you want to come with me to help me pick out the person?"

Me: "No. I'll wait here. Are you going to the bar up the street?"

Terrance: "Yeah."

Me: "Okay. Be careful."

There was a bar up the street from our house where Terrance and his friends liked to go. I was not feeling going out tonight, but he knew what I liked. It was not our first rodeo. At the house chilling in a nightgown that is sexy yet still covered up, I was watching the television, and sipping a little Don Julio chased with pineapple juice.

About an hour or two later, I hear Terrance keys jangling again. He walks in with his best friend, Jason. I assumed he did not see anyone worthy enough, so I left it alone. We were all talking, laughing, and drinking. I had turned the television off and we were listening to music. Terrance grabs me by my waist, pulling me toward him as we begin to dance.

Jason: "I love y'all relationship," Jason sips his drink while giving me an amorous look, "Y'all dope as fuck. I have to get me a *Tara*."

Me: "I'm regular. Ain't nothing too fancy about me."
I shrugged my shoulders. We all giggled as Jason walked into the bathroom.

Terrance: "Babe, let's try something a little different." Terrance suggested.

Me: "Like what?" I responded.

Terrance: "Never mind. Forget that I mentioned that."

Terrance walked toward the refrigerator. I gave Terrance a suspicious look.

Me: "Yeah, I think we should leave it alone."

Jason: "Aye, Tara, is it okay if I spend the night? I don't want to get a DUI." Jason has a job that requires him to have an excellent driving record.

Me: "I'm not tripping. This Terrance's house, I just have a key to everything."

Jason: "Thanks. I appreciate y'all."

Me: "No problem."

Terrance and I head to the room. Of course, his horny ass is hot and ready like Little Caesar's. His arms are around my waist as he is lifting me to the bed. I flopped down and slid my nightgown up. I threw one of my legs up, gripping the back of his head and ears as I twined his face. My eyes close as I embrace the moment, legs shaking as my first round was coming out. Terrance reached for the long red blindfold, covering my eyes, and tying the material behind my head. He pulled up the restraints from the bottom of our bed and bound each of my wrist and ankles. He kissed my lips, licked my earlobe, then slid his tongue down my neck.

Stroking my breast, he repeatedly flickered and rotated his tongue down the center of my chest. Just as he was about to go down, he jumped off the bed. I heard the door open and close slightly. I assumed Terrance went to grab something tasty from the kitchen. He loved adding things during fourplay. A moment later, my thighs were gripped, followed by kisses and suckles in my inner thigh. It felt different but better than Terrance's usual touches. I am riding his face, and his moans reach louder peaks than mines. Talking in tongues, he speaks out,

"Damn, your pussy is so tasty and pretty. How do you make it taste like that?"

Me: "What the fuck? Uncuff me right now!" I jerk and yank in anger .

Terrance: "Tara," Terrance unlocks my restraints, "Don't go crazy on me."

I reach for the blanket, trying to cover up. Things had suddenly become very entangled and uncomfortable. In another life, I would have been okay with Jason talking in tongues, but in the current time and day... Jason was Terrance's best friend. I could not do that.

Jason: "Tee, I thought you said you talked to her." Giving Terrance a small shove.

Terrance: "I did, but I didn't give her all the details." As he leans on the dresser.

Me: "What details?" placing my glass down.

Terrance: "This is the threesome I want." Walking toward me .

Me: "Whaaat? So, y'all gay?"

Terrance: "Hell, nahhh. We are not gay. We just both want to have sex with you." We all laughed.

Me: "So, you are okay with me fucking your best friend?"

Terrance: "To be honest, I know that he liked you before he introduced me to you at his birthday party. We both wanted you and did not know who you would choose. So, we played our position and waited. You put him in the friend zone. So, I stepped up."

Jason: "Tara, I've been wanting you for a while. I respect y'all relationship, but I'm attracted to you as well in like a real way."

I mean, honestly, I never told Terrance, but I wanted Jason in the beginning. Terrance was more consistent and convenient. Jason's job always had him on the road, but I sometimes wish I would have pursued him first. *Shiiit!* Fuck it. There was a first time for everything. What about the double standard? Two girls and a guy are a threesome, but two guys and a girl is supposed to be a train. It did not feel like I was losing in this situation. I was getting the best of both worlds.

Of course, other thoughts were going through my head. I was going to pay attention to everything, I wanted to make sure they stayed focused on me. I was not sure I could handle things crossing over into something I was not ready to see. The opportunity to have sex with Jason was right in front of me, and I was going to take advantage of it. I also wanted to teach Terrance a lesson.

I grabbed Jason by his shirt and slammed him on the bed. I got on top of him and started kissing on his neck. Grinding on his dick as I kissed him, it rose to the occasion. With one knee bent, I push my right leg out a bit and slid his dick inside of me. I rode that dick like I was a professional rodeo rider. I spun around while Jason's dick was inside me, looking Terrance in his eyes as he stood back and watched. I let my eyes roll to the back of my head as I start moaning like crazy.

Terrance storms away in anger. I keep going. Bouncing, grinding, rotating, and moaning louder and louder. I wanted Terrance to hear it from the next room.

Jason: "Oooh, fuck!
Damn, Tara.... hold up.
Wait, wait, wait."

Knowing Jason's about to cum, I give him three more bounces and hop off. He explodes then runs to the bathroom. I heard two doors slam back to back. Terrance had left the house—his house. How can he be mad? It was his idea, right? You better know your role .

Issa Fetish

It was a warm sunny day in the city. Ladies were out, wearing maxi dresses with and without panties, and guys had their shirts off. It was a nice day to head to the beach. I was walking into the grocery store when some guy yells out to me.

Him: "Excuse me."

I turned around, attempting to move out of his way.

Him: I'm trying to get your attention," he laughed.

Me: "Oh, I'm sorry. I thought I was in your way. What can I do for you?" Placing my hand over my heart.

Him: "You're very beautiful." Eyeballing me from head to toe.

Me: "Thank you." I smiled.

Him: "Oh, my gosh. Your feet are so beautiful." He gives a mesmerize stare.

Me: "Thank you." Blushing.

Him: "I'd love to take you out sometime and get to know you. May I have your number?"

Me: "Sure."

He pulls his phone out, and I put my name and number in it. He is dark skin with a medium build and the same height as me. Right away, thinking in my head, I cannot wear heels with this guy.

Me: "What's your name?"

Him: "Daniel, but I go by Dee."

Me: "Nice to meet you, Daniel. I'm Tara."

He grabbed my hand and kissed it as he looked at my feet again, shaking his head.

Dee: "Maaan, you have some sexy ass feet."

Me: "Thank you *again*," I giggled, walking into the store.

I grabbed the items needed and head to the beach, where I spend the day chilling with my friends, catching

up, eating, and reminiscing. As the sun is setting, and I prepare to leave. I am rinsing my legs and feet with water bottles when I look up, and I see Daniel.
Dee: "I didn't know you were here. I would've come and chilled with you, or we could've walked the beach and got to know each other."

As he is talking, he takes the towel from around his neck and starts to dry my legs and feet.

Me: "That's sweet of you, but you don't have to..." Placing my hand on his shoulder, attempting to stop him.

Dee: "No, trust me, it's an honor." Dee looks up smiling.

Me: "Thank you." As I let him proceed to dry my feet and rub them at the same time.

Me: "You better stop that, or I will expect you to do that all the time."

Dee: "I don't mind." As he finished.

We talk for a little while, then I had to go. Before I left, we planned a date.

Dee: "So tomorrow at noon, be ready." Dee shouts out as he walks away.

Me: "Okay. It's a date." As I give a friendly wave .

The next day, I prepared for my date with Daniel, not knowing what we were doing or where we were going. Dressing casually, I wore some denim shorts, a comfy but cute shirt that hung off my shoulder, and cute sandals, with a clutch to match. We went to lunch, then he asked if I would like to go back to his place and chill. At his house, we are talking and getting to know each other a little more. He reaches out and grabs my ankles, putting my feet on his lap. Sliding my sandals off, he begins massaging my feet as we talked. Grinding my feet on his dick at the same time.

I will admit the massage and the feeling of his dick felt so good. As I was speaking, I mean literally mid-conversation, he picked up my left foot and placed my big toe in his mouth. Sucking it as he caressed it. Running his tongue down the center of the bottom of my foot and I jerked my leg back. Not that I did not enjoy it because I did, but I was ticklish and suddenly very horny. As he is sucking my left toes, I'm rubbing his dick with my right foot.

I knew I was ready for intercourse, but I liked him. I wanted to make him wait a little longer. Get to know him better, so everything was not based on just sex. I stopped him and told him I had to go. As I get up, he grabs my hand.

Dee: "You didn't like that?" he asked curiously .

Me: "Trust me, I did. I just have something I have to do that's time-sensitive."

Dee: "I understand." As he walks me to my car.

I had been busy with work and had not gotten a break. Even sleep had been hard to come by. I had a huge project that was indeed time-sensitive and especially important. I had to give it my all with no distractions. While at work, a delivery guy comes in with a bouquet of flowers and a gift box that includes some gorgeous high heels. I read the card:

> *"You always keep them nice & neat,*
> *Sure, as hell makes me weak*
> *here's a foot massage—my treat,*
> *And some heels for your feet."*

Yes, cheesy as hell but creatively different. I gave him an A for effort. After work, I went and got my foot massage, which ended up being a full body massage because they catered to more than just my feet. Daniel loved showering me with gifts. Especially heels, sandals, foot massages, and pedicures. My boo could not get enough of my feet. I was done with my project, and it was back to reality. I was ready to break Daniel in, so I give him a call.

Dee: "Hey, queen."

Me: "Hey, handsome. What are you doing tonight?"

Dee: "Nothing, just cooking up some dinner. About to chill and watch football."

Me: "Oh, do you have company? I can call you back."

Daniel normally hosted Monday night football at his place with the guys.

Dee: "No, the guys went to a bar, but I'm chilling at the house tonight."

Me: "Oh, okay. Give me a second. My other line is beeping. I'll call you right back."

Dee: "Okay, love."

I hop into the shower and oil up. Smelling good wrapped in my long beige peacoat, along with the heels he just bought me, I head over to Daniel's house. I cut my headlights off and turn the music down as I turn on his corner. Creeping up the driveway, I call his phone. He answers...

Dee: "Took you long enough, babe, I thought you fell asleep on me."

Me: "Unlock the door."

Dee: "You're kidding me."

I can hear him grinning as he is walking fast to greet me. He opens the door with shock on his face. I pushed him out of the way as I stepped inside. Locking the door, I turned slowly and disrobed, wearing nothing under my peacoat. Daniel picks me up and spins me around with excitement before leading us to his room. He threw me on the bed and immediately started sucking on my toes. He is passionately moistening my body from neck to toes with his tongue.

Catering to each toe. As he slid inside me, he guided my feet to rest on each of his shoulders. As he is thrusting his dick, he's moving my feet to rest on his face. Grabbing my ankles, he buries his face in the center of my feet as if they were hands, with my legs in a butterfly position. Constantly sucking my toes, his dick is growing harder and harder with every suckle. I am about to cum. How was he doing this?

"I'm about to cum.
Fuuuuuuck!
Oh my... oooooh...."
Daniel's grunts are massive.

"Yeeesssssssss!" I scream as I nutted all on his dick.

I do not know what it was with him and my feet, but I knew he intensely fetishized them.

Maybe It's Fate

It was the first day of summer, and anyone from California knows what that means. Get them cars washed, hair done, fly 'fits, nails fresh, and hopefully that body is tight and ready. Time to hit "The Shaw." The Shaw, also known as Crenshaw Boulevard, was where you go to hang out, have fun and show out. Pull up and parking lot pimp. We always started somewhere around Rodeo Road (now known as Obama Boulevard) to 120th Street, but traffic had changed over time.

It became Sunset Boulevard to Compton Boulevard and Main Street, then Western Avenue and Manchester Avenue to Broadway and Imperial. Follow the traffic and move when the police show up. If you get lost, call a friend or someone you just exchanged numbers with. It had always been a thing in California. People are happy, friendly, and social, but that does not mean it is safe. Be careful. Shootings and robberies happen, too. I have lost a few family and friends to the streets, but this is not a sad story. So, let us get started...

I like being around wild people sometimes. It was more fun to watch than being on the front line. An associate of mine, Nikki, had texted, asking me to come over to her house.

Nikki: Come through bitch. My mom's cooking and I know your greedy ass want some and then we can hit the Shaw tonight.

Me: Okay. Come pick me up in an hour.

Nikki: Alright .

Her mom be throwing down in the kitchen, so when I got to Nikki's house, I was tearing the food up. Around midnight we freshen up and hit The Shaw. We are cruising down Crenshaw. Riding, flirting, and exchanging numbers. Nikki is plus-sized, cute, and keeps herself up, but she deals with a few insecurities about her weight. She likes to use me as bait. While I'm conversing with a guy, she uses it as an opportunity to holler at his friend. I just want her to live life to the fullest, so I don't mind as long as it works for her.

As we were riding, Nikki has her eyes on a prize. A light-skinned, fly, pretty eye guy with long wavy hair. She tries to catch up to him, but each time he gets away. Driving like a bat out of hell was an understatement. She was determined. The sun was coming up. Traffic was dying down, and people were starting to turn it in.

Me: "Let's go to Denny's on Coliseum. My treat," I suggested.

Nikki: "Okay. Let me put some gas in my car first."
Nikki turns into the Arco.

As we were leaving the gas station off Jefferson and
Crenshaw, guess who we see... *You damn right!* Nikki
hauls ass to catch up, and as she is pulling beside him,
he is just laughing.

Light Skin Guy: "Why are you driving like that? I almost
shot you," He lowers his weapon.

Nikki: "Because I've been trying to catch you all night,"
Nikki uses the baby voice she puts on for the hotties.

Light Skin Guy: "Well, you got me now, so what's up?"

Nikki: "Lemme suck your dick!"

Light Skin Guy: "Whaaaat?" He laughs.

Nikki: "Pull over. Lemme suck your dick," Nikki licks
here lips as she adjusts herself in her seat.

My eyes grew big, but it was none of my business.
She wanted him bad, and she is a grown-ass woman.
We pull over a block away from the Denny's parking lot.

Nikki: "What's your name?" Nikki ask as she is
consistently blushing.

Light Skin Guy: "Boss." He fumbles through his phone with brief eye contact.

Nikki: "Boss, lemme suck your dick."

He walked over, and Nikki got up so he could sit in the driver's seat of her car with his feet still planted on the ground. She began sucking his dick, and I kept myself entertained by texting while she did her thang. I could not help but glance over from time to time. She did her shit!

Boss: "Damn..." Boss cradled his cock smiling while he kept nodding.

I could not tell you all the tricks she pulled or the moves she made, but I knew he was impressed after she was done. As they are exchanging numbers, Boss looks over at me.

Boss: "What's your name? I got somebody for you."

Me: "No, thank you," I laugh.

I did not want whoever he "got for me" to think they would get the same type of treatment. The assumption that just because you associate with certain people that you had to be like them. It was not always true.

Boss: "I want you to talk to my lil' bro. His name Lil' Boss."

Me: "No, I'm okay. I'm really happy with the guy I'm with." I was saying anything to get him to ease off me.

Boss still got on the phone and called Lil' Boss anyway.

Boss: "Where you at, stooooopid? I got somebody right here for you. Pull up to Denny's on Crenshaw. Come through."

Apparently, Lil' Boss was in bed or occupied. He was not about to pull up at 6 a.m. to see some female. It was music to my ears.

Boss: "You want his number?" Boss skims through his contacts.

Me: "No." Giggling as I shook my head .

Boss: "Well, if you change your mind, tell Nikki to get at me."

Me: "Okay," I roll my eyes as I laughed him off.

Who would have thought that giving head on the first night would turn into something long term? Nikki loved her some Boss, and he loved her, too. She was always so excited when she saw him. She called me up to give me the tea almost every time she saw his lil' homie. Steady telling me about how Lil' Boss was so fine and how I needed to give him a shot. I was not into the whole matchmaker thing.

Me: "Enjoy your boo. Long as you're happy, I'm happy. Oh, but when the time come I'ma want some pointers on the sloppy toppy. Whatever you are doing, bitch, I need to take notes."

Nikki: "I got you."

We both laughed. Fast forward about six months later...

On my lunch break I decide to go to Jack in the Box around the corner. As I am driving, I feel like I am being followed. Keep in mind, I am working overnights. So, it is late. Every time I make a turn, the car behind me is making it, too. I only get a thirty-minute break, so I proceeded to the drive-thru. I knew they had cameras just in case something happened. The suspicious car pulls in right behind me. I am looking through my rearview and side mirrors. I see him staring and smiling, flirting through the mirror.

Not going to lie. He is handsome. So, I am enjoying the eye candy, but at the same time he was just driving recklessly behind me. I get my food and head back to

work. Because it is late, we lock the gate and must input a code to pull back in. I am about to enter the digits when the same car pulls up behind me. I am nervous and trying to think fast. *Should I continue or stay on the outside so the patients and the rest of the staff will remain safe?* I decide not to unlock the gate
yet.

Me: "Can I help you?" I yelled out.

Eye Candy: "Yeah. What's your name?" He approaches my car.

Me: "Why? What's your name?" I ask in suspense.

Eye Candy: "My name Lamar, but you can call me Lil' Boss."

Me: "Where have I heard that name? Who sent you here?"

Lamar aka Lil Boss: "Nobody. I saw you checking me out in the drive-thru, so I figured I would be nice and come give you my number. You left before I could say anything."

Me : "This is you being nice? A little arrogant, I see."

Lamar aka Lil Boss: "I'm handsome, you're beautiful. We belong together. Don't you think so?"

Me: "Let me answer that after we get to know each other," I give Lamar my number, "I have to get back to work."

As I pull into the gate, I can see my coworkers looking through the glass door. Nosy asses could have opened the gate from the inside and let me in but wanted to witness whatever could have happened instead. Lamar and I talk on the phone from sunup to sundown. My lunches are usually spent with him. Rest breaks, before and after work, we are talking on the phone and seeing each other anytime we can. We are both greedy, so we go out to eat a lot. I am really falling for him.

We have sex often. It is passionate and good. I think we were trying to turn each other out. He brings out the inner slut in me, and I bring out some in him, like it was meant to be or something. One day Lamar asks me to pull up. He was out with some friends, and I had just got off work. I had chilled for a few but was ready to go. Lamar asked me to follow him. As we are driving, I am noticing we are not going to his home or mine, so I call his phone.

Me: "Where are you taking us?"

Lamar: "Follow me back to my other spot."

Me: "Other Spot?

I never knew he had another spot—*sneaky tail*. That is another conversation though. All I know is that my mouth is horny, and I want him now.

Me: "Pull over right here. I'll park my car and get in with you," I direct him toward the Food4less parking lot.

Lamar pulls over, and I get in. I unzip his pants and pull his dick out while he is driving. Considering the notes, I took from Nikki, along with what I have learned through voyeurism, I am going in. Gurgling, spitting, juggling balls, deep throating, and flickering my tongue on his scrotum. Two hands, one hand, no hands. His cum aimed right at my tonsils. It felt like the horse game at a carnival, the one where you squirt water through the hole to make the horse get to the top. He is driving fast to get me to "his other spot." We finally get to his apartment in Long Beach, off Paramount Boulevard. As I walk in, I hear the television.

Me: "You left your TV on?"

Lamar: "Nah, that's probably my roommate."

Me: "Roommate?"

Lamar has passed hints about threesomes and different things. I hoped he was not going to be on some kinky shit. I was too tired to put on a show. As I walk further into the apartment, I see his "roommate" sitting on the couch.

Boss: "Ain't that a bitch. You act like you was too good for my brother." Boss laughs.

Me: "What the hell? That is crazy." I'm shocked and giggling.

Lamar looks at me with disgust, probably due to his brother's "track" record.

Lamar: "How the fuck you know my brother?"

Boss: "Remember ole girl, Nikki, I told you that gave me that bomb ass head near Denny's?" Boss grips his crotch laughing "That's her homegirl that I was tryna plug you in with."

Lamar: "Ooooh," Lamar laughed, "So it was destined for her to be my lil' slut."

Boss: "Yup, that shit was meant to be."

Boss gives Lamar a high five and I grab Lamar by his belt buckle pulling him toward the room "Maybe it was fate."

Meaning To My Passion:
My Rider Intro

Before I go on, I should let you know why I have chosen my promiscuous route. For the record, I am not looking for acceptance, but to simply open your mind to the idea of knowing a situation can make or break you. I have chosen to allow my past to turn me into a savage. This lifestyle is not for the weak. Which brings me to...

My Rider...

My Rider

I had just gotten out of a toxic relationship. I am talking about real love/hate relationship. Like the Bobby and Whitney mixed with the Ike and Tina kind of love/hate... without the drugs. He was my first everything. I could not tell you what another dick or tongue felt nor looked like. He was all I knew. Over the years, he tore me down— mentally, physically, emotionally, and spiritually. Getting away from him was one of the best things to ever happen to me.

Yet, I was lost. He had stripped me of my confidence and had me questioning my self-worth and value as a woman. My self-esteem was dead. He told me no one would want me with stretch marks, the extra weight I had put on and being a single mother. He said the only reason anybody would fuck me is just to get even with him, and in his mind, it would take away from any value I had left as a woman.

I believed him because so many people disliked him. Maybe his enemies were just after me to say, "That's why I fucked your bitch,"— *in Tupac voice.* He had my mind all fucked up. After I left him, I started suffering from depression. When guys would try to talk to me, I would not allow anyone in. I could not stop reminding myself of all the psychotic things he had planted in my head.

"They just wanna fuck. They don't see me for me. I have stretch marks. Guys don't date girls with stretch marks. I'm a single mother. What could they possibly want with a woman raising a child on her own?" I kept saying all that to myself.

Slowly, my confidence began to grow. It took a lot of self-healing, meditation, and time. I felt like an upgrade of my old self. I was stronger—physically, mentally, emotionally, and spiritually. I was working out, in school, had a good job, and had a better connection with a higher power. I knew I was beautiful inside and out. So, I started hanging out again, but a confident woman with a scorned heart is a powerful yet dangerous combination. A close friend had repeatedly asked me to go out with her. I kept telling her no for a long time. Eventually, I started dragging myself out and showing my face in the world again.

We went to a few night clubs, strip clubs, motorcycle clubs, and Sunday Fun Day, watching people race and have fun. My face became familiar to some, and their faces became familiar to me. When we would go out, I would see this tall, dark-skinned guy with a stocky build named Rider. In most eyes, he was the man in these streets. He has the money, the expensive cars, the motorcycles, the boats, and the hoes. I knew he was an active gang member, and from what I had heard, a good reputation for certain things in that nature as well. In urban terms, "HE WITH THE SHIT." Honestly, all those features turned me on.

Admiring him from a distance because I am not feeling what comes with it. I mean, he was cool, but I did not like the way females flocked to him. They probably did not know anything about him as a person. Just what he had. During my time of growth, I noticed that most people only dealt with certain individuals because of what they had or the reputation they carried. Just to brag about bagging someone with a nice car or a little money.

It was like they wanted the specific person that the streets talked about. They do it for the hype and really believe they are the "chosen one" if they get to sleep with them. Only to later realize that person was screwing any and everything that came their way. So, no one was special. In this type of world, you were either doing the fucking or getting fucked over. I am watching and trying to never fall victim to these shenanigans.

One day my close friend, La'Nae, asked me to be her wingman. She had been telling me about how her guy friend had a brother who had been asking about me. I did not want to, but for my friends, I would go against the grain...sometimes. I mean, what is the worst that could happen? I am just entertaining someone while she gets a little action in. Riiiight? I do not have to sleep with nor marry the guy.

As soon as we pull up, there were a lot of guys at the house. They immediately start hovering around my car. I am kind of nervous as I hurry up and push my purse under my seat. I did not have much, but I did not want to get robbed either. La'Nae's phone rings, and she quickly tells me she will be right back. She had been anxiously awaiting to tend to her guy friend. As soon as she gets out, I lock the doors, crack my windows, and leave the car running.

"What did this girl get me into?" I mumble to myself.

The whole-time different guys keep coming up to my car, whispering through the window and trying to shoot their shot. Nothing but corny pick-up lines until one guy just came right out and was like, "You should fuck with me, I trick on my bitches."

I thought, *Really? This is how society is greeting women now? I guess I haven't missed out on much.*

I am irritated as hell, but I want La'Nae to get her time with her boo. I spot a guy heading toward the car, and as he gets closer, he yells, "Get the fuck away from her car, blood." They all scattered like roaches. I was surprised the savages that had been hounding me listened. When he approached me, he was calm and polite. He asked if I would like anything to drink while I wait? I told him I was fine.

Him: "My bad for my homies. Some of these fools never had pussy before, and some of them never saw a female as beautiful as you. So, they don't know how to act."

We both laugh.

Rider: "My name is Rider. What's yours?"

Me: "I'm Tara."

I already knew who he was as soon as he got up close, but it didn't hurt to play dumb sometimes. I had the time anyway since I was still waiting on La'Nae. A little small talk never hurt anyone.

Rider: "I've seen you around, and I'm always asking for you, but you always seem to leave before I could get close enough to speak." Rider leaned on my car.

Me: "Is that right?" I giggled, blushing as I saw the sincerity in his eyes.

We picked each other's brains about all types of random stuff as he stood outside my car, still talking through the crack of my window.

Rider: "Can I get in? I'll sit in the back if you want me to."

Me: "As if that'll make me feel safe. Let me see your ID. I'm not letting some guy with an alias of "Rider" in my car."

He slipped his license through my cracked window as we were both laughing.

Me: "I guess you can sit down, *Anthony*," I unlock the door.

Rider: "A whole hour passed, and you were going to keep me outside.I guess they don't make 'Gentle*women*' anymore, huh?"

Me: "I guess not. I'm concerned for my safety, fuck everything else."

Rider: "Don't worry. I'll always protect you."

Me: "I'ma hold you to it."

As we continued to talk, I realize he is not as bad as I thought. He had a little book smart to match his street smarts. La'Nae came back to the car, blushing a couple of hours later.

Rider: "Can I have your number so we can continue where we left off?" Anthony pulls out his phone.

"5...6...2—"

Me: "Shut up, heffa," I cut La'Nae off, "How you know I wasn't going to give him a fake number?"

La'Nae: "By the way y'all was smiling when I walked up, I thought you gave it to him already."

Me: "What my number or something else?"

La'Nae: "Your number, nasty."

I have always had a slick mouth. I like to find ways to turn any conversation into a nasty one. I talked dirty, but of course, my mouth was always clean—just a little harmless fun. I gave him the rest of my number.

Rider: "I'll call you later, beautiful," he reaches to receive his phone back.

Me: "Okay," blushing as I hand him his phone.

I dropped La'Nae off and got settled at home. As I was getting out of the tub, I see a missed call from Anthony, so I returned it.

Rider: "What were you doing?" He asked inquisitively .

Me: "Just got done playing with my pussy in the tub."

Rider: "All this time, I'm thinking you're a good girl and you a lil' freak."

Me: "I don't like that word. It's so judgmental," I laugh.

Rider: "Why?"

Me: "Because I believe a freak has no limits. There are some things I just wouldn't do and plenty of things I haven't tried yet."

We started elaborating more on things we have tried, things we want to try, and things we should try together. Anthony did not know it, but he was about to become my playmate. My ex was my first and my only. For the most part, sex had been basic. I did not have much experience, but I fantasized about it all the time. I was ready to let the fun begin. On our first encounter, he got a room. The romantic scenery helped to break the ice. We had candles, balloons, soft music, massages, and flowers. He did his thang. I was beginning to feel special and sexy again.

Fast forward to his dick game. I always thought dicks were the same size and widths with different complexions depending on age and nationality. I was totally wrong. It felt good, though. He was so much bigger than my ex. This dick was working with some heavy artillery. Like I just went from a .22 to a 9 milli, mixed with that .38 special—and I am lusting after this .38 special. We had so much sex, and each time he taught me something new about my body and different ways of giving and receiving pleasure.

Helping my pussy to adjust comfortably to his penis size. Anthony stayed giving me compliments. Telling me how my toes curled each time he twisted and rotated his tongue on my inner thigh. How my pussy grips his dick even tighter when I am trying hard not to cum, only to massively explode all over his dick. He taught me to pay attention to details during sex, so I learned what made him weak in the knees. How he always tried to change positions when he felt like I was out fucking him. The difference in fucking, making love, quickies, and rough sex.

A good student eventually becomes the teacher. More importantly, I knew how to change his mind and stay with me when he was about to be up to no good in the streets. Let us just say I have saved a few lives or at least spared them—for a little while, I hoped. I loved that he was spontaneous. Unless I was angry or being professional Anthony was *My Rider*. So, I had no problem calling him Rider. We had been down a few years. Official, yet still non-official. I did not want to be labeled as his girlfriend, and he respected that. But that was my man. I am talking about really riding together until the wheels fell off. He made sure I was always treated right and respected. I could call him for *anything*, and he knew he could do the same in return. From changing my tire to fixing something around the house, whatever I wanted or needed. Oh, and of course if somebody disrespected me or tried anything, he was there. Male or female, he was riding with me. He had my back. No matter how big or small, Rider was my *Rider*.

We had become so comfortable with each other, but sex was my focus. We had random sex almost everywhere you could think of. The hood of my car after we pulled over near a warehouse factory, and the back seat of his car. His house, my house, his granny's house, hotels all around California, in the bathroom, on his boats, and in bedrooms at friend's houses. We went to Dockweiler Beach and had sex on top of the Baywatch Tower. Even if we had not intended on being around each other that day, once we discovered we were at the same location, we always left together. Separately, of course. I was a private person, so we agreed that it was our little secret.

Only certain friends who were always around us knew what was up. They also knew to keep their mouth closed. So it was that extra zing because some had a feeling, but not too many could ever prove it. Until one evening... I went with my girls to a party in Baldwin Hills that ended up being his friend's party. It was a crazy coincidence. Anthony had *way* too much to drink that night.

As I was coming out of the bathroom, he catches me in the hallway. He creeps up on me from the back, wrapping an arm around my waist from behind, giving my neck and ear a quick lick. Acting on reflex and instinct, I pushed him off me as I turned around, angry, and about to react. It was dark throughout the house. Plus, Rider had some sneaky, disrespectful, and rude friends. I would not put nothing past them.

I turn and see that it is him. We were kissing in the hallway and making our way into one of the rooms. He has my hands overlocking and raised up above my head as he pins me against the wall, rubbing his dick on my pussy. Slow grinding and turning me on even more. Rider is kissing my neck as he is grabbing and rubbing my ass, lifting my legs up occasionally. He pulls my pants and panties down, then twists and rotates his tongue on my inner thigh. Knowing I loved it when he did that shit, I slid my sandal off and wiggled my right leg out of my pants and panties. He put a hand under the back of my right knee, lifting my leg. There was a nightstand next to me that I used to prop my leg up, giving him all the room, he needed—and he went to work!

Just as I am getting into it, someone bursts through the door. "Oh shit, my bad!" A female starts to excuse herself until she looks again, "What the fuck? Just friends, huh?" She yells before leaving and slamming the door. I did not know who the girl was, but apparently, Rider did. He starts apologizing and saying he had something to tell me. By the look on his face, it was serious, and he was nervous as fuck. He starts sweating, and now I am nervous.

Me: "What's wrong, Rider? You good?"

Rider: "No, Tara." he smacks his hand on the wall in anger.

Me: "What's wrong? Who was that?" I shout, pondering apprehensively.

Rider: "Maaan.... fuuuuuck!"

He yells, then punches a hole in the wall.

Me: "What the hell is wrong? What's da deal, Anthony?"
I started putting my clothes and sandal back on. Rider grabs my face, lifting me up by my chin. Then he places one palm of his hand on each of my cheeks. Squeezing them to make my lips pucker. He kisses my forehead and then my lips.

Rider: "Tara, I love you. I will never stop loving you."

Me: "I know, Anthony. What the fuck is going on? You are about to have me wild out. What's good, man?"
I went from being worried about him to upset.

Me: "What the fuck is it already? I hate dramatic ass scenes."

Rider: "Tara, the bitch that walked in on us is about to have my baby," giving me a look of great sorrow.

Me: "Wait... what?" I felt like a knife pierced my heart
Rider: "I was gonna tell you sooner, but she was back and forth on if she was going to keep it or not. So, I

didn't see a reason in telling you because I didn't want to lose you, especially over a possibility."

Me: "You know what," I smack my lips, "I'm not tripping. Technically, we are not an official couple anyways. So, I cannot be mad at you. It is what it is, but I'm about to head out."

Rider: "Nahhh... you stay here. I'm about to make her leave."

Me: "No, it's cool. My homegirl is ready to go, and she rode with me, so I have to take her home."

Rider: "Wait a minute. I'm riding with you then."

Me: "Noooo...I just need a minute. Our communication was always better than that, but you are slacking on your shit. The fact that you did not feel like you could talk to me about this lets me know we're not as close as I thought we were. On top of that, you're out here barebacking bitches."

Rider: "I'll give you that. I am sorry. My bad, Tara, just please come back. It happened one time."

The look on his face said he knew I was not coming back. His pupils were dilated, and his sclera were bloodshot red, and he was sweating in cold weather. He began to show so much rage. He squeezed my upper arms with both his hands tight, then he grabbed my jaw and chin area as he yelled at me.

"BLOOD... YOU BETTER COME BACK. I TOLD YOU THIS BITCH IS ABOUT TO LEAVE. DON'T MAKE ME COME LOOKING FOR YOU, TARA!"

The female looked at me with envy in her eyes before she started walking to her car in tears. My homegirl came up and pulled me away from him as tears ran down my face. I had seen him trip and go off on other people but NEVER on me. My arms and jaw were still throbbing, and my heart was racing. All I could think about was the abuse from my ex. After that, my heart went numb. From that day forward, I refused to allow any man to get close enough to hurt me again. I have my will power back, and I am officially in control.

I am a boss. I can do everything on my own, and what I cannot do, I will pay someone who can. I cannot go down that road again. This must be the end.

...Or perhaps it won't be?

About The Author

Gitara George is a humble mother and entrepreneur raised in Compton, California. She takes pride and dedicates herself to helping others and trying to rebuild the community. She owns The SeKret Doors, an online adult store, and SeKret Trips, a company that transports families to prisons across California. She is also the founder and CEO of a non-profit organization, The Village of Blessings. Writing poetry and sexual skits have always been her hobby and stress reliever, and now she gets to share them with the world. **Connect** with the author on Instagram: @Lilmstara or sexperience.info818@gmail.com

The SeKret Doors
Visit thesekretdoors.com
Follow @thesekretdoors on Instagram
Like @thesekretdoors on Facebook
Or send an inquiry thesekretdoors@yahoo.com

Village of Blessings Nonprofit
Visit villageofblessings.org
Follow @the_village_of_blessings on Instagram
Or send an inquiry thevillageofblessings@gmail.com

Sekret Trips
Send an inquiry to sekrettrips@gmail.com